THE FATAL CHORD

THE FATAL CHORD

OR

THE BAFFLING MYSTERY OF THE ODEON MURDER

Written by:
Albert Payson Terhune

Edited by:
Trudy Thomas Monteith

To George —
A great
friend
Trudy

First Edition 2023

This book is an edited reproduction from a 1904 newspaper. Every effort has been made to reproduce the original text however, due to the age and condition of the newspaper, there may be occasional differences which in no way impede the reading experience.

ISBN 978-0-9649321-1-1
Library of Congress Control Number 2023909106

Trudy Thomas Monteith
Tiger Press
TTMstlBOOKS@gmail.com

ACKNOWLEDGMENTS

I would like to acknowledge and thank Albert Payson Terhune (December 21, 1872 – February 18, 1942) who, in 1904, introduced The Englishman and provided yet another exciting mystery solved by the "world's greatest detective."

I also thank Michael W. McClure of Baskerville Productions for his support and encouragement. His suggestions were quite helpful and greatly appreciated.

And, especially, I thank my wonderful husband, Harry Monteith (aka Harry Monti), who is by my side in everything I do and has been supportive and encouraging throughout our 52 years of marriage. Thank you, Tiger! I love you dearly.

PREFACE

"Magic" has been my whole life. Fifty-two years ago, I married, the love of my life, Harry Monti, one of this country's premier close-up magicians, and we have had a truly "magical" life.

I began researching the history of magic in St. Louis dating back to the early 1800s and, in the course of that research, I discovered a story that I "presumed" to be a Sherlock Holmes mystery, *The Fatal Chord, or the Baffling Mystery of the Odeon Murder.*

It was written by Albert Payson Terhune and published in the *St. Louis Post-Dispatch* in twelve installments from April 11, 1904 to April 23, 1904, and all landmarks mentioned in the story were specific to St. Louis.

However, while doing further research on the St. Louis story, I found that Mr. Terhune also published another version of the same mystery in *The Evening World* (New York, New York) which ran from April 4, 1904 to April 16, 1904, entitled *The Fatal Chord, or the Baffling Mystery of the Carnegie Hall Murder.* That storyline was identical to the previously-mentioned *Odeon Murder*, however, all landmarks in the *Carnegie Hall Murder* were specific to New York.

As of May 15, 2023, the website *Historical & Fictional Characters in Sherlockian Pastiches* indicated that *The Fatal Chord, or the Baffling Mystery of the Carnegie Hall Murder*, had not been published since

1904 and was not published as a book. I have since published it as a book in June 2023.

The location of the novel you are about to read, *The Fatal Chord, or the Baffling Mystery of the Odeon Murder*, is St. Louis. The Odeon Theatre and Masonic Temple, as it was called, was located at 1042 North Grand Avenue.

The storyline provided by Albert Terhune, whether in St. Louis or in New York, immediately introduces the reader to the "world's greatest detective" and, though he does not specifically mention the name of this detective . . . it must, of course, be Sherlock Holmes. But, was it really Sherlock Holmes? I leave it to you, the reader, to determine for yourself if "The Englishman" detective so wonderfully introduced by Mr. Terhune is actually Sherlock Holmes.

Please . . . read on!

Trudy Thomas Monteith
(aka Trudy Monti)

TABLE OF CONTENTS

CHAPTER I

THE STORY OF A CRIME

Two men lounged in the big black leather chairs in a corner of the Southern Hotel lobby. It was Sunday morning. Groups of frock-coated, silk-hatted guests loafed about the lobby, reading the voluminous Sunday papers, chatting in knots, or strolling to and fro in the broad corridors.

A uniformed porter was pushing an irregular line of sawdust before him across the marble pavement with a long brush.

Through the broad front doors and windows poured a flood of morning sunshine.

The two men in the corner regarded their surroundings with diametrically opposite emotions.

One of them, a big, thick-set fellow, who, despite his correct Sunday costume, looked as though he would have felt more at home in a blue coat and helmet of a policeman, was impervious to the scene about him. It was an everyday matter to him. The panorama seen through the glass of front doors and front windows means nothing to Detective Sergeant John Gresham.

With his companion, it was otherwise. This second man gazed eagerly, with an almost childish delight, at everything. His appearance differed from his companion's, almost as utterly as did

1

the feelings with which he looked out on the typical Sunday morning scene on Broadway.

He was Charlie Beckwith, known (at first contemptuously and later admiringly) as "The Millionaire Detective." Born to the purple, he had wearied of the vapid life of the average St. Louis society man and had turned his attention to the detection of crime. His natural aptitude along the line had been so strong that he had at last won the reluctant admiration and respect of that conservative body, the "chief's office."

As he was rich, well-born, and clever, his odd trade did not, strangely enough, imperil his position in society.

"If you only knew what a treat it is to get back to God's country, after six whole months on the other side!" he was saying to his companion. "There isn't a lamppost or street corner in little old St. Louis that I don't want to say 'Hello!' to."

"What time did you get in?" asked Gresham, vastly bored by this rhapsody.

"Not till nearly 12. That's why I'm up so late this morning. It's awfully good of you to drop in to welcome me."

"Oh, I thought you might like to hear what's been goin' on since you left. Get the papers I sent you?"

"Yes. Thanks very much. I didn't miss a great deal of fun by being away. The Barrel Murder was about the biggest thing that happened while I was gone.

"I'd have liked to see what I could have made out of that. Anything new since I sailed from London?"

"Anything new?" echoed Gresham, amazed. "What's the matter with the Ballard case?"

"Ballard case?"

"You haven't heard? Staying so long on the other side has dulled you. A man in our business can no more afford to miss his morning and evening papers than a Fourth Street man can afford to neglect his ticker."

"Well," laughed Beckwith, good-humoredly, "now that you've said your piece, maybe you'll relent and tell a poor foreigner something about this wonderful Ballard case. Who is Ballard? A Monk Eastman impresario or a bank cashier with a more than neighborly interest in the safe's contents?"

"Neither. He is – or he was – Cyril Ballard."

"Not little Cyril Ballard of Kirkwood? You don't mean to say that little cad has had brains enough to win criminal laurels?"

"That 'little cad,' as you call him, has the bad luck to be dead."

"Dead! When? How?"

"When? Friday night. How? No one knows. If he was poisoned, the autopsy failed to prove it. He fell dead. That's all."

"Heart failure, probably. There's no mystery about that, as far as I can see."

"That's like you amateurs. Always jumping to conclusions before you've heard half the story.

"There's only one thing worse than jumping to conclusions too quickly, and that is jumping to them too slowly."

"I'll be good," said Beckwith with mock humility.

"Now go ahead and tell me the story."

"There was a musical in the Paul Craddock's rooms at the Odeon. Craddock had invited a lot of people to hear the new piano genius everyone's raving about."

"Siurd Von Rickerl? I've read about his success. He's a good fellow. I know him well."

"That's the man. It seems Von Rickerl had just composed a concerto or a sonata, or a song without words, or an oratorio, or a fugue, or a barcarolle, or whatever name musical folks give to these measly pieces that have no tune, and he was to play it in public for the first time at the Boston Symphony concert yesterday at the Odeon. Craddock and he are old friends and Craddock induced him to give the piece its initial performance at Craddock's rooms. A lot of musical guys and some society people were invited there to hear it. Well, while the crowd was standing around before the playing began, Cyril Ballard fell dead."

"How did it happen?"

"The piano stood in a sort of alcove, separated from the drawing room by portières. When the music should begin these curtains were to be swept back. Von Rickerl had never tried Craddock's piano and he was just starting into this alcove to test the instrument's tone before playing, when the little Ballard chap, who seems to have been doing fresh things all evening, butts in ahead of him and sits down at the piano and begins to strum on it.

"Von Rickerl was riled I suppose, for he stepped back. But he says that just as he did so, he noticed that some other man besides Ballard was in the alcove. He didn't notice who this other man was. Ballard, as soon as he found that Von Rickerl was not following him, must have left the piano and started back through the portières into the drawing room. He struck one heavy chord on the piano. Every light in the place went out and then flared up again. There was a sort of smothered yell, and Cyril Ballard rolled through the curtains onto the drawing room floor stone dead."

"Well?" queried Beckwith impatiently as Gresham paused.

"Where's the mystery in all this? If we lived 30 centuries ago his death would be explained on the grounds that the outraged God of Music had slain the outsider who outraged melody. As we're in the twentieth century, I fall back on the suggestion of heart failure. And now that I remember, Ballard was a victim of chronic indigestion. He was always boring us at the club by talking of his ailments and hauling out a bottle of pepsin tablets and offering some to us. He used to munch pepsin as girls munch candied violets. I suppose this indigestion tackled his heart at last and then he died."

"I'm not through yet. Say, Beckwith, I'm not making a report to Chief Desmond or giving an interview to the newspapers. I'm telling a friend a story and I'm going to tell it my own way. If you don't like it, you can chase over to a newsstand there and get a Sunday *Post-Dispatch* and read a terse account of the tragedy. But if you're going to listen to me, you've got to stop springing theories on me before you know what I'm driving at.

"It's a pleasure to be able to ramble on once in a while without having to collect all my facts in a bunch and throw them at my listener. So give me elbow room."

"Fire away, old man; I won't stop you again," adjured Beckwith, and Gresham resumed:

"Now here's where the queer part of it comes in.

"There was the usual panic and excitement and all that sort of thing, and a doctor was sent for, and two or three men leaned over Ballard, and tried to revive him. Then, all of a sudden, the room turned pitch dark for a fraction of a second. And through the

darkness, everyone heard the piano give out one deep crashing chord. The very same chord that Ballard had struck just before he died. Then the lights flared up, and it was seen that not a soul in the room was within ten feet of the piano. Now what do you make of that?"

Gresham paused triumphantly. Beckwith stared at him open-mouthed.

"A trick!" he hazarded.

"Then how was it played?" asked Gresham. "Who could have plunged that big room into total darkness, duplicated that one big chord on the piano, then turned up all the lights? How could he have accomplished the whole trick in the merest fraction of a second and without going near the piano? Just tell me that."

"No chance, I suppose, of a trick of the imagination? When people are excited ..."

"At least 50 people agree on the story. If one hysterical woman or one scared man had fancied the lights went out and the piano struck that chord, I wouldn't believe it.

"But a whole roomful couldn't be deceived that way."

"Go on," said Beckwith briefly.

"Well, after the second panic had been checked and the people induced to get out quietly, and the doctor pronounced Ballard dead, it was up to the coroner."

Gresham bit off the end of a long black cigar, struck a match, puffed gravely for a moment, and then went on.

"The coroner, McCree – one of the new ones, you know – had an acute attack of conscientiousness. He ordered an autopsy. He also made a discovery."

"From the autopsy?"

"No. Before it.

"On the floor, where it must have rolled from Ballard's vest pocket as he fell, was a little bottle, half full of brownish tablets."

"Those were the pepsin tablets I told you about.

"He was always taking out that bottle and chewing away at the pepsin."

"You win. It was the pepsin bottle, all right. But McCree insisted on having some of the tablets analyzed. The first tablet tested was pepsin; the second, though, contained only a fraction of pepsin. The other ingredient was some sort of silicate, whose nature and effects none of the local chemists can yet determine. There were 12 tablets left in the bottle. Four of them bore the trademark of the firm that put them up. The other eight were shaped like them but had no trademark. Those eight held the mysterious ingredient. That was enough for McCree. He ordered the autopsy."

"What did they find?"

"First of all, that the man had not died of heart failure. There were no lesions about the heart and no rupture of the coronary arteries. The whole organ, auricles, ventricles, and all, was in perfect condition. Moreover, no traces of poison could be found from any of the ordinary tests they applied to the stomach's contents. That would seem to confute McCree's poison theory. A more elaborate test is being made but with no results thus far."

"But ..."

"Do you know what the coroner thinks Ballard died from? From fright! Sheer fright. He says the state of the heart and nerve indicate it. He declares Ballard died from the effects of a terrible and sudden fright."

"But what on earth could have scared the chap? He had good nerves. What could he have seen or heard there in that crowded drawing room to scare him to death?"

"No one knows. That's the mystery, that and the sudden moment of darkness and the crash of sound from the piano. But I'll swear I never before saw such a look of abject horror as was stamped on his face. A very pretty mystery as it stands.

"If we were back in Puritan days, we'd whisper, 'Witchcraft!' And it surely does seem supernatural."

"Pardon me, Sergt. Gresham," observed a man who, unobserved by the two, had been reading and smoking in a big lounging chair just to the left of the detective, "but if you are not careful you will set fire to your cuff, just as you did a month ago. And, as your laundry did not come home yesterday evening when you expected it, you would have to go without cuffs until tomorrow. It is a pity that your parents disapproved of your smoking."

Gresham had indeed, in the absorption of the talk, been holding his cigar bent downward (a habit of his) in such a way that the ash was rubbing against the edge of his cuff. A moment more and the linen must have been burned.

He looked the newcomer over, with the cold insolence which is the true St. Louisan's birthright and which the average man resorts to when unwarrantably addressed by a stranger.

"Thanks for calling my attention to it," he said curtly. Then, nettled at the other's comment, he added:

"I'd have been more grateful if you hadn't rung in that business about my accident last month. I'm sick of being guyed about it. Who told you?"

"No one," was the somewhat bored reply. "I merely saw that you were about to set fire to your cuff. I noted a narrow semi-circular scar from a burn running part of the way about your wrist, evidently caused by just such an accident. My knowledge of surgery told me that the scar is barely four weeks old. It was quite simple. As simple as my knowing that your laundry did not come last night."

"How do you make that out?" grumbled Gresham suspiciously; while Beckwith seemed on the point of going into a paroxysm of silent laughter over some joke whose point he alone saw.

"Easily enough!" replied the stranger. "I saw that your cuffs were reversed. Now, a man so careful in dress as you evidently are would not resort to reversing his cuffs as long as he had a clean pair to put on. If he were out of clean cuffs, he would buy some, unless he expected his laundry to come home that same day. Finding (last night when all the haberdasher shops were closed) that your laundry was delayed, you decided to reverse your cleanest cuffs today, that is all.

"As for your parents having disapproved of your smoking, that is still simpler. A boy who is afraid his parents will catch him smoking always holds his cigarette downward, sheltered by his palm. It is a habit that usually lasts through life."

"Say!" cried Gresham, admiringly, "you ought to be a detective."

"From time to time I've done a little in that line," admitted the stranger modestly.

"Gresham!" cried Beckwith, unable to keep the secret longer. "Let me present to you a man whom you've always held up as your ideal detective."

"What!" exclaimed Gresham, leaping to his feet.

"Do you mean to tell me this is Sherlock Holmes?"

"Do you mean – Sherlock Holmes?"

CHAPTER II

THE FAMOUS DETECTIVE

Gresham repeated incredulously, "Sherlock Holmes! Are you?"

"Am I Sherlock Holmes?" finished the stranger.

"That's a question many people have asked. You can answer it to suit yourself. Here are the facts: A great English writer has created the character Sherlock Holmes and imputed to him a certain skill in unraveling knotty criminal cases. Now it may be merely an odd coincidence, but Sherlock Holmes's methods and many of his strangest adventures are the methods which I credit myself with originating and the adventures which I have experienced."

"In other words, you are the original from whom he drew Sherlock Holmes," completed Beckwith. "It was in that way Dr. Watts introduced me to you in London."

"Say," interrupted Gresham, "sizing you up from your picture and the way you talk, I believe you are Sherlock Holmes himself and that you're concealing your name to avoid notoriety here."

"Think what you like," replied the other in a tone that made Gresham wonder whether or not this tall, thin man was having a joke at his expense or whether he was in earnest. "I've told you I am supposed by many people to be the original Sherlock Holmes. It is also true I came here to rest and to avoid notoriety."

"If you aren't really Sherlock Holmes, then what is your name?" queried Gresham. "I know most of the big English detectives by hearsay. What is your name, Mr. Englishman?"

"Well," drawled the stranger, with an amused glance at Beckwith, "suppose you keep on calling me The Englishman."

"So be it," agreed Gresham with a rather woeful laugh. "But I suppose your wonderful skill as a detective is genuine, even if your name isn't, eh?"

"I can vouch for its reality," laughed Beckwith.

"I had the honor of meeting 'The Englishman' in London, and he let me accompany him on one or two cases. His work made me feel like a raw beginner. How furious poor Dr. Watts was because a broken leg laid him up and 'The Englishman' did me the kindness to choose me as his companion on those two expeditions! Then we came over together on the Cymric, and ..."

"Are – are the stories written about Sherlock Holmes all true?" asked Gresham, staring at his hero as a newsboy might at Jeffries.

The great detective's brow clouded slightly.

"There are very interesting stories," he replied, "but there is a tendency to look on the romantic, sentimental side of every case and to play that up at the expense of some of the finer details of work. There is no poetry, no romance in our business, as you know."

Knowing how sore a subject this was to The Englishman, Beckwith hastened to change the topic.

"I'm thirsty," he announced. "Let's all go across the hall to the café and I'll proceed to demonstrate to you how infinitely superior a Scotch highball is to a British brandy and soda."

"I must apologize, Sergt. Gresham," said The Englishman as he sipped reflectively his long, golden drink, "for eavesdropping. I saw Beckwith talking with you and came across to speak to him. I found you were telling a most interesting story, so I sat down to wait until it should be concluded. I read of this Ballard case in the *Post-Dispatch* last night. It is as interesting a case as has come under my observation in some time."

"It's the most complicated mystery of the year," asserted Gresham warmly.

"Mystery?" mused The Englishman, frowning slightly.

"Is there such a thing on earth as a mystery? Show a baby the alphabet. It is a mystery to him. Yet a little study makes it clear as day. Show an unthinking man some of the facts in a crime and he will declare it a mystery. Yet, invariably, a little study will make it clear. The word 'mystery' has no place in our language."

"Mystery? . . . Is there anything such as a mystery?"

"Then kindly explain the Ballard case to me," retorted Gresham, somewhat nettled.

"I have not studied it. I qualified my assertion by saying that 'study' should make all mysteries clear. For instance, here is something that might seem mysterious to some people: You left your watch at home this morning. It is a gold stem winder, and you wear it on a fob. Not on a chain.

"Your fellow detectives make fun of you for having a fob instead of a chain. You carry the watch in your left-hand vest pocket instead of in the right, like most people. You did not forget it this morning, but left it home purposely."

"That's all true," agreed Gresham, grinning in a puzzled fashion, "but how you knew it is a mystery!"

"That same old word 'mystery' again. It is no mystery. Nor, if the truth were known, is the Ballard case."

"Would you mind telling me," asked Gresham, more respectfully, "how you came to all these conclusions about my watch?"

"By calculating the faculty of observation. That is all.

"I knew you left your watch at home because as we came into the café you felt for it and it was not there. You felt at the left side of your vest, not the right. Your hand touched the vest just below the center of the left-hand pocket. That is where one would reach for a hanging fob. The hand goes higher and nearer the center to catch a chain. That explains what I said about the left pocket and the fob.

"When you found the watch was not there, you did not look worried, as one would who had forgotten to wear his watch and who could not, for the moment, think where he had left it. You remembered at once that you had left it off purposely. That it was a gold watch and a stem winder I deduced from the rest of your costume. A man as careful about his dress as you are would have only a first-class watch. Your clothes are up to date. Such men do not carry cheap or old-fashioned watches."

"How did you know the other men at the chief's guy me about the fob, though?"

"You ought to know that half the watches reported stolen are really only lost, and that they are lost because they are on a fob and not on a chain that would hold them in case they slipped from the wearer's pocket. This fact made the police avoid wearing fobs, and they usually make fun of anyone who is so foolish as to wear one. They would be doubly amused at one of their own companions who took such risks. As you see, it is all absurdly simple. And so this Ballard murder will prove, as I said, with a little study."

"Study!" groaned Gresham. "Every copper and detective and reporter in St. Louis is spraining his brain to study it out. And we can't make anything of it."

"Perhaps you've all been studying with your books held upside down. For instance, what examination – microscopic examination – was made of the floor in that part of the alcove where Herr Von Rickerl said he saw a man standing at the time Ballard thrust his way into the alcove? I suppose the floor was hardwood? Yes? And from the curtain being drawn across, few guests would probably go in there. So a boot mark on the waxed floor might have been visible to the microscope. It might have led to the identifying of the one person who was near Ballard when he died. "I suppose no such examination was made?"

"None," said Gresham, "it isn't the custom here."

"Nor in England, except in such cases as I undertake. Still, it is just in such tiny details that the key to these alleged 'mysteries' is found. Footprints only discernible through a microscope, flakes of tobacco ash, even the half-invisible mark made by a brushing shoulder or fingertip, on a wall or door. All these are significant to the trained observer. Tell me," he broke off abruptly, "did you personally examine this alcove?"

"Yes."

"There is no door leading from it into any other room?"

"None, it opens only in the main drawing room.

"I even examined the walls of the alcove.

"They are papered and there is no chance for a secret door in the wall. Besides, it's in a modern studio building where such things would be impossible."

"What furniture is in the alcove?"

"None except the piano."

"You are absolutely certain? No chair, nor even a hassock or a tabouret?"

"Not one stick of furniture except the piano; I'll take my oath on that. What's the joke?" – for a smile was relaxing the tense lines about The Englishman's lips.

"Merely a question of observation. You, a skilled detective, stand ready to swear there is not an atom of furniture of any sort, except the piano, in that alcove. Yet what was the pianist supposed to sit on while he played? Was there no piano stool?"

Gresham bit his mustache with vexation.

"I'd forgotten the piano stool," he said sulkily, "but I can't see what bearing it has on the case."

"Most probably it has none at all. I merely mentioned it to show how seldom the police take the trouble to get all the details accurately. A man in your business should be able to photograph in his brain everything he sees at such a time. This man Ballard, was he married or single?"

"Single, rich, and stingy," put in Beckwith. "When I left St. Louis six months ago, there was some talk of his being engaged to an Italian girl, an artist named Bona Pittani, whom society had taken up. There was no doubt the girl was head over ears in love with him, though what she could see to love in ..."

"Oh, that was off some months ago," interrupted Gresham. "It can have nothing to do with his murder."

"An Italian girl deeply in love – the man does not marry her - can have nothing to do with his murder. Oh, these police!" muttered The Englishman under his breath.

Then aloud:

"Had anyone a grudge against him? A motive for his death? You say he was rich and unmarried. Who was his next of kin?"

"His brother, Royce," answered Beckwith.

"Their father was a millionaire. Cyril was his favorite son. Royce was wild, and there were some shady stories afloat about him. He was a ne'er-do-well. Never stuck to anything. Studied medicine – was expelled. Took up law – failed. The father left his fortune to Cyril, leaving Royce just enough to keep him going. There was little love lost between the brothers."

"Studied medicine, eh?"

"Oh," cried Gresham. "You think it was he who made those tablets? We never thought of that. You think he's the man?"

"I think nothing because I know nothing of the circumstances. What was it you said to Beckwith a while ago about the folly of jumping to conclusions?

"But, if I might offer a suggestion, look up this Italian girl's career since she broke up with Cyril Ballard, and also try to find the extent of Royce Ballard's knowledge of medicine – especially of chemistry. The host – Craddock, I think you said his name was – what sort of man is he?"

"He's all right," responded Beckwith quickly.

"He's an odd chap, one of the stern, quiet, masterful sort, with a tremendous lot of force and personal magnetism. But when you get to know him, you see what brick he is. He's one of the few Bohemians left in St. Louis. Not the sort that wear long hair, forswear the bathtub, frequent 30-cent table d'hôtes, and fail to pay their debts; but an all-around citizen of the world, accomplished at everything and a man who bends society to his will instead of bending to society's. He's been everywhere, done everything, and knows everybody. By the way, when I left he was rumored to be engaged to Iris Durand. I wonder if it is true?"

"I guess not," answered Gresham. "I don't know people in that walk of life, of course; but I read in one of the society papers just a little while ago that a girl of that name was reported engaged to this piano chap, young Siurd Van Rickerl."

"She's a lovely girl," said Beckwith. "I wish them luck. But," changing the subject, "this Ballard case, Mr. Englishman, is just the sort of thing I should have thought would wake you up wise. It may not be a 'mystery,' but it surely has points that promise to be of interest. Why not take a fly at it?"

"I came over here for a rest," objected The Englishman. "I was run down from overwork. Besides, I don't know your country or

your city. In England, I am at home. Finding a criminal there is like finding some familiar article in my own room. Here it is all strange to me. I should probably fail. I certainly could not do myself credit. And yet ..."

He paused.

"It's a grand chance, "urged Beckwith. "It's the greatest case of the year. You will get a grand chance to study our police methods, to see St. Louis, and to meet a lot of pleasant people. Think it over."

"No need to think it over!" sighed The Englishman, regretfully. "I came here for rest, but the moment I read of that case last night in the *Post-Dispatch*, I felt the old fever of the man-hunt rushing back on me and I knew there was no use trying to shake it off. I say, there's 'no need to think it over,' for it's all thought over; I shall take up the case!"

The Odeon Theater

Gresham and Beckwith thrust out congratulatory hands.

"It'll be an honor to work with you," exclaimed the former.

"It is I who am working with you, not you with me," corrected The Englishman.

"Remember, though, in introducing me that I am Dr. Joseph Watts, not the man you believe to be the original Sherlock Holmes. And first of all, let us go to Craddock's rooms. It may not even now be too late to pick up some clew there."

CHAPTER III

INTRODUCING SEVERAL LOVERS

T he second of Mr. Paul Craddock's exclusive and brilliant
'musicales,' as the society papers termed it, was in progress.

The first of these musical evenings, which the death of Cyril
Ballard had so tragically interrupted, was to have had as its chief
feature the initial rendition of Siurd Von Rickerl's new opus
"Alaaschar."

Tonight, a month later, the same inducement was offered.
Despite the memory of that tragedy so recently enacted there,
many members of St. Louis's artistic and musical circles, as well as
of its society circles, eagerly welcomed the opportunity to throng to
Craddock's rooms at the Odeon.

Paul Craddock was a man who only semi-occasionally
entertained. When he did so, the occasion was usually one not
lightly to be missed for Craddock had reduced to a science the art
of successful entertaining. People who went to his "affairs" were not
forced to talk to uncongenials, but were allowed to do pretty much
as they pleased. Craddock seemingly took no especial heed of their
doings, yet all the time contriving to set everyone at ease. There
was, too, always some especial attraction offered there.

The host, a man of perhaps 40, powerfully, yet lightly built, a
pointed black beard lending a foreign air to his dark, strong face,

stood out from the crowd of guests as a striking figure which would command chief attention everywhere. He had the nameless air of distinction which nothing but centuries of high breeding can give and which is (falsely, as a rule) attributed to royalty.

His deep-set eyes swept the rooms, seemingly without purpose, until they rested on a woman's profile, thrown into cameo-like relief for a moment against the dark red portières of a bay window that concealed the rest of her figure. With apparent aimlessness, Paul made his way through the group of guests, reached the bay window and, drawing aside the portière, sank into the cushioned window seat at the girl's side. She had looked up quickly, eagerly, at his approach. On recognizing him, a slight cloud, imperceptible to less keen eyes than Paul Craddock's, had crossed her face.

Craddock at once divined that she had been waiting there for someone else, for someone whose presence would have been far more welcome. Tactfully, he made no allusion to this, but entered into casual talk.

"It was good of you to come tonight, Miss Durand," he began, "and to brave the sad memories that the sight of my room must bring. I was half afraid no one would venture here after the tragedy that stopped my last little musicale. It must be doubly hard on a sensitive, artistic nature like Van Rickerl's."

"Mr. Craddock," said the girl impulsively, "I came here tonight more for a word with you than for the music."

"Yes!" interpolated Paul, courteously, as she hesitated. "You were waiting here in the bay window for me?"

"No." she answered frankly. "I was waiting for Siurd Von Rickerl. I knew he would come here to look for me as soon as he arrived."

"That isn't very complimentary to me," said Craddock, with a smile, "but a girl with eyes like yours could not lie. Yet you said you wanted a word with me during the evening. Pending Von Rickerl's arrival, perhaps you'll ..."

"Mr. Craddock," she interrupted, "I don't like to bring up the subject. It is not pleasing to either of us, but ..."

"Let me save you the trouble, then. Some time ago, I begged you to do me the great honor to be my wife. It meant a great deal to me. You may not believe me when I tell you that, though I have reached 40 years, you are the first woman I ever asked to marry me. I only mention this to show you that mine was not a mere passing love, but one that filled and mastered my whole being. It was the first emotion I ever had that ruled me. All that cannot be of interest to you. But it would perhaps explain and palliate what followed. You did not, could not, regard me as anything more than a friend – a good, loyal, devoted friend, I trust – and you told me so, very kindly but very honestly. You even told me your own heart secret – your secret betrothal to Von Rickerl. That should have been enough for me, but it was not. Like a fool, like a raw, senseless schoolboy, I begged you, on the night Ballard died here, to reconsider your decision."

The girl glanced up protestingly, but he continued:

"When you refused, I lost myself for the moment, for the first time in ten years. I have a fearful temper. It is the one thing on earth I dread, and for years I have been able to keep it under control. But that night, all the world seemed to crumble away, and I lost hold of my temper. I told you that I was stronger in every way than Von Rickerl, that I could make a woman of your splendid type happier than he could. I even sank to the wild threat that I would prevent your throwing yourself away on such a man. I rehearse that scene now to punish myself still further; though the shame and self-

contempt it gave me have never been for a moment absent from my heart since then. My words were those of a coward, of a cur. I not only insulted the woman I most honor in all the world, but I spoke slightingly of the true man whom I am proud to call my friend. It was to ask an explanation of all this that you wished to speak to me tonight, was it not?"

His earnestness, the evident humiliation of this proud man, usually so strong, so silent, appealed to Iris Durand even more than did his words themselves. She laid an impulsive hand on his arm, and the light touch thrilled him like a chord of wild music.

"Don't," she begged. "It is horrible to hear a man like you speaking that way of himself. There is nothing more to be said about it. I understand, I think, and if you want my forgiveness, my continued friendship – they are both yours without asking. Please let's keep on being friends, and let's both forget anything unpleasant that's happened."

"Thank you," said Craddock simply. The unwonted emotion had passed from his face, leaving it, perhaps, a shade paler than usual. "Thank you," he repeated. "I ..."

Then, as his quick ear noted a slight stir in the main drawing room, "Ah, Von Rickerl must have done. I'll go and speak to him. I ought not to have left my guest so long."

He rose and left her. She looked after him wistfully. "How splendid and strong he is!" she murmured. "The sort of mysterious great-hearted man women adore and make a hero of. Perhaps – if I'd never met Siurd ..." Her sentence was unfinished, for a second man paused before the half-closed portière.

"Siurd!" she exclaimed, rising and, concealed by the shadow of the curtain, grasping the newcomer's hand in both of hers. "I thought you were never coming. What detained you?"

The newcomer, a slender, tall man, with big blue eyes, a boyish face, and a shock of yellow hair, answered with a slight German accent:

"I'm sorry I kept you waiting, Liebchen. I dined with Charlie Beckwith and an English friend of his, a Dr. Joseph Watts. We all came here together. Have you waited long?"

"Siurd! I thought you were never coming. What detained you?"

"Only a few minutes. Did you enjoy the dinner?"

"Very much. You always liked Beckwith, and I like to hear stories of his adventures in his role of 'Millionaire Detective.' His

friend, Dr. Watts, I didn't care for especially. He is a quiet, stupid-seeming fellow."

"He must have some brains or Mr. Craddock would never have taken him up as he has. Mr. Beckwith introduced Dr. Watts to Mr. Craddock, and I've seen them together several times this past month. O, look!" she broke off suddenly, nodding toward a man who had just entered the drawing room.

"There is Mr. Royce Ballard! To think of his going out like this, barely a month after his brother's death. He is cold-blooded. He cares for no one. Least of all did he care for his brother. He doubtless comes here to show his contempt for poor Cyril's memory.

"Mr. Craddock is beckoning you. Don't be nervous, dear, when you go to the piano. Put that tragedy out of your mind."

As the lovers left the bay window a man slipped into the window seat. He leaned far back into the shadow as though to avoid the observation of someone, and over his shallow, dark face an annoyed expression settled.

"Thank heaven, the music's begun," he muttered half-aloud. "That'll keep her from wandering around while it lasts, and the minute it's over I'll get out. If I'd had any idea she'd be here tonight ..."

His chivalric reverie was interrupted. A woman slipped noiselessly behind the portière and seated herself beside him on the window seat.

"My dear Royce," she whispered maliciously, "did you really think you could evade me? I have written to you, tried to waylay you, and in every way sought an interview since your lamented brother's death, but you have refused. Why?"

"Because there is nothing to be said between us," growled Royce Ballard. "There is ..."

"There is a great deal to be said. There is everything to be said," she cut in vehemently. "When you induced your brother to break his engagement with me you promised to marry me. Do you think I am the sort of woman to be cast aside like that?"

"Nonsense. Bona. Don't make a scene. I'm too poor to marry."

"But you are coming into your brother's wealth when the estate is settled. I ask you once more: Do you mean to keep your word?"

"And marry the fair Bona Pittani, whom my brother jilted? Scarcely."

"You – you lied to me then? You ..."

"Don't talk to me now, please. I want to listen to Von Rickerl's playing."

"You cur! You would put me off like this? Deceived me into believing you were to marry me, and then throw me away like an old glove? If ..."

"My dear Bona! Can't you see you're spoiling all my enjoyment of the music? If you don't stop talking I shall be obliged to move out into the room."

Do!" she hissed, furiously. "Do, and I swear I will denounce you before everyone here!"

"Denounce me for failing to relish the notion of marrying my brother's cast-off sweetheart? I leave you to imagine which of us would suffer most from such a scene."

He had risen and took a step toward the rest of the guests. But Bona laid a detaining hand on his arm. The fury had cleared from her face.

"No," she said. "Don't leave me. I know how low, how despicable a thing you are, and yet ... and yet, God help me, I love you. I can't let you go like this. Be a man. Be your better self. Redeem your pledge to marry me. No other woman in all the world would adore you as I do. Ah, Royce, give me but the chance and I will prove ..."

"You're attracting attention to us," he retorted angrily. "Let me go."

He caught the white detaining hand that clutched his sleeve and wrenched it loose with a brutal force that almost wrung a cry of pain from Bona.

The gesture transformed her in an instant from a pleading, passionate woman into a devil.

"Go, then," she whispered hoarsely, "and at the first step you take I will cry out denouncing you; not of winning and casting away my love, but of ..." She whispered a half dozen words in his ear. The effect was electrical. Royce Ballard sank back, pallid and shaking, into his seat.

"It's ... it's a lie!" he murmured feebly.

"What wretched luck!" muttered a man who leaned lazily against the outer side of the portières, not two feet away. "Just as it was growing interesting, she spoke so low I could not hear a word she said."

It's – It's a lie!" he murmured feebly.

CHAPTER IV

ON THE TRAIL

For a full minute, Royce Ballard sat as though paralyzed by the news he had just heard. When he spoke it was in so low a tone that the unseen listener could not catch the words. But a few moments later his voice rose somewhat.

"Don't you suppose I've thought of that?" he was saying. "I knew that anyone who suspected might try to search my rooms for it when I was absent. I carry it with me all the time.

"There is no evidence that will let them arrest me and search my clothes. But any third-rate detective - yes, or any woman with a grudge against me, for that matter – might gain access to my rooms in my absence and find it. That's where I was wise."

"You say no one had evidence against you that could warrant your arrest? How about me?"

"I didn't know until tonight that you had any knowledge of the ..."

"You know it now. My dear Royce, with me for an enemy you are lost. With me as an ally, you are safe and a millionaire. The price of my alliance is a plain gold ring. A wife cannot testify against ..."

"You have conquered," he growled, sullenly. "I'll marry you. But," with a snarl of irrepressible rage, "I'll lead you a dog's life. I'll make you curse the day you forced me into this hateful union. I ..."

"I'll take my chance on that, Royce. The woman who can make you cringe before her and agree to marry her can take pretty good care of herself afterward. They're applauding. I'm really sorry to have missed Herr Von Rickerl's music, but the talk we've just had is worth it. Shall we join the crowd that is congratulating him? Eh?"

Bona had stepped through the half-drawn portières but shrank back with a little gasp.

"What's the matter?" asked Royce, uneasily.

"Why, a man's leaning against the wall right by the edge of the bay window, within two yards of us! How much do you suppose he heard? I thought everyone was across the room nearer the piano."

Royce lifted a corner of the portière in the direction she indicated and took a long look at the man. Then he dropped the curtain with a sigh of relief.

"It's only that stupid Englishman, Dr. Joseph Watts, Beckwith's friend," he said contemptuously. "He's leaning there with his eyes shut and his mouth open and his silly head nodding. Music's charms seem to have 'soothed his savage breast' to slumber. Even if he'd been awake he hasn't enough sense to understand us."

"Can he have been listening while he pretended to be asleep?"

"If he was, he'd have moved away the second we discovered he was there. No, Watts is a 'negligible quantity.'"

"You're sure? He gave me a scare. Who is he, anyway?"

"An Englishman who scraped acquaintance with Beckwith on the other side. Beckwith seems to think he owes him something, for he takes him everywhere, even in his researches into the cause of Cyril's death."

"Is Mr. Beckwith on that case?"

"Yes. He is always meddling in other people's affairs. To justify his idiotic nickname of 'The Millionaire Detective,' I suppose. There's nothing to fear from him. No more than from this stupid Watts fellow."

The 'stupid Watts fellow' meanwhile gradually awoke from his doze and strolled over to where Von Rickerl stood by the piano.

While seemingly deeply absorbed in the musical discussion going on there, he did not fail to note that Bona Pittani and Royce had emerged from the bay window and had joined the other guests. Taking an envelope from his pocket, The Englishman quietly tore off the superscription and, stepping near to Royce, let the envelope fall to the floor.

"Excuse me, Mr. Ballard," he said, stooping to pick it up, "but I think you have dropped something."

Royce made an involuntary upward movement of the right hand toward his breast pocket; then, seeing that what The Englishman had picked up was merely a torn envelope, he glanced carelessly at it and said:

"No. It isn't mine."

"Good!" murmured The Englishman to himself.

"This 'something' that he carries with him all the time for fear of its being discovered is in the left breast pocket of his coat or his waistcoat. But how to get at it? And what is it? Whatever it is, it has

bearing on his brother's murder. If I were back in London there are a dozen of my assistants who could help me get possession of it. As it is, 'this stupid Watts fellow' may possibly outwit the clever Mr. Royce Ballard after all."

For some time past, The Englishman had been quietly but intensely busy. Introduced by Beckwith as an English friend who was interested in watching American methods of detective work, he had accompanied the "Millionaire Detective" on the latter's investigation of the Ballard case; had examined carefully the body, and, as far as Craddock would permit, the surroundings in the latter's apartments at The Odeon, where the crime had been committed. Here, however, he had encountered an unexpected and irritable obstacle.

Craddock had calmly refused to have 'a gang of thief-takers prowling about his rooms,' as he termed it. Any reasonable investigation, he said, he would permit with pleasure. But he saw no reason why measurements, microscopic examinations, etc., should be made. The law did not demand them and he refused to permit such intrusions.

The Englishman, by admitting that he was a detective, might, of course, have obtained the necessary permission from the authorities. But he did not choose to jeopardize his future success on the case by throwing off the incognito of 'Dr. Joseph Watts' unnecessarily. He knew that dozens of persons had tramped about Craddock's rooms since Ballard had fallen dead there and that their careless footprints had doubtless blotted out all significant traces of the crime's origin and originator.

Moreover, there seemed, in view of such probable obliteration, no absolute necessity for such a search. Yet The Englishman was resolved at the first good opportunity to make it. Though realizing that each passing day made the chance of a 'find' there more and more unlikely, he was determined to make, sometime, such a thorough microscopic investigation of the apartment as his soul craved.

With this object in view, he had sedulously cultivated Craddock's acquaintance. To most of the people who had met him through Beckwith, The Englishman seemed uninteresting, self-absorbed, and somewhat stupid. Craddock, however, who saw far deeper into human nature than did those about him, read 'Dr. Watts' differently. He saw the tremendous energy, the keen, analytical mind beneath the difficult exterior, and he felt an unwonted attraction toward the famous sleuth. He and The Englishman were much together.

The great detective, on his part, was keenly interested in Craddock. Here was a man who, with all his great powers of deduction, The Englishman could not make out, subtle, brilliant, honorable, contemptuous of his fellow men, secure in the knowledge of his own power. Thus, he had sized up Craddock's complicated character.

Thus, indeed, he described him to Beckwith as the two detectives walked homeward down Grand Avenue late that night.

"He's the sort of man who stands head and shoulders above the average," answered Beckwith. "In times of panic or trouble, the rest flock to him like frightened children to a father. He has good nerves, too, to sleep in that place after the awful tragedy that happened there. Especially after the seemingly superhuman events that accompanied it. By the way, have you formed any theory to account for that instant of utter darkness and the crashing out of that one loud chord from the piano?"

"Not yet," answered The Englishman, "but if I were not hot on another trail I should have formed a theory to account for that and

for certain conditions I noted about Ballard's body and which the police and the doctors alike seem to have overlooked. But that theory was so wild, so utterly improbable – and besides, I had no chance to verify it by proper examination of the room and ..."

"Would you mind telling me the nature of this 'wild theory' you at first formed?"

"No – yes, on second thought. I'd rather not until the affair is solved. Then I'll tell you of any of my false clues that may interest you. In the meantime, the probabilities are in favor of our fixing the crime on our friend, Royce Ballard, as you expected."

Briefly, he recounted the events of the evening.

"This Pittani girl," he finished, "has some strong hold over Ballard. As I take it, she – and she alone – has proof that he killed his brother. The secret of that crime he carries in his breast – not figuratively – but in his breast pocket. I found that out tonight. My next move is to search Royce Ballard and find out what this secret is. It may be the chemical formula for the poison. It may be some of the poison itself. It may be some incriminating document. In any case ..."

"But the analysis failed to show any marks of poison in the body, and those mysterious brown tablets, when analyzed, contained no known poison."

"None known to local chemists, you mean. I have sent to my laboratory in London for certain tests of my own invention which I mean to apply to those tablets. The tests should be here in a few days. I flatter myself that they will lay bare the most subtle poison. When I find the nature of the poison, I will also know its effects. Then it will be an easy matter to have the body exhumed and see if our suspicions are correct. But a surer and far simpler course will

be to obtain the paper or whatever it is that Royce Ballard says he carries night and day. And that is what I am going to get."

"But how?"

"Gresham can get me a blank warrant and I fancy I can make up sufficiently well as a detective to ..."

"You mean you'd arrest him on some trumped-up, fake charge and go through his clothes?"

"No, no; I wouldn't go through his clothes. They'd do that at the nearest station house to which I brought him. I'd examine the papers, find I had the wrong man, and let him go. That's all."

"But it's illegal. It's ..."

"When you're dealing with a criminal you must meet him on his own ground if you hope to win. Tomorrow I shall get the warrant and put my little plan into execution.

"May I count on your help?"

"If any other man asked it I'd say 'no,' but you can count on me in everything. I'm with you, though it will involve queer work before we're done."

CHAPTER V

AMERICAN METHODS VS. ENGLISH

Shortly after noon on the following day, two men walked through the Southern Hotel lobby toward the Broadway entrance. One was Charles Beckwith, the other a grizzled man with a square jaw, bushy brows, and respectable but ill-fitting clothes.

His oldest friends might have gazed long and keenly at this second man without recognizing the scrupulously dressed, well-groomed Englishman.

Habitués of the hotel, accustomed as they were to seeing men of this appearance with Beckwith, scarcely gave a second glance to the pair.

"This disguise is wonderful," Beckwith was saying, admiringly, "and made with so few alterations, too."

"That is the art of it," responded The Englishman.

"The perfect disguise is almost no disguise at all. The average amateur seems to think that the more coverings he heaps on his face the better he hides it. So he claps on false whiskers, goggles, paint, and all that. And anyone who knows the game can detect at a glance that the man is disguised. That isn't my line. I have studied disguises for nearly twenty years, and the best of all is one that is

practically no disguise at all. To look at me you would be puzzled to detect any artificial change I have made in my face."

"That is true," said Beckwith, scanning him closely. "But your bearing is different. You wear your clothes as if they were ready-made. You walk heavily and there is a slouchy, unkempt air about you. You've touched up your hair a bit to give it a grizzled look, but your face is not made up. It is only the difference of expression that changes it. You look like an honest, plodding, rather unintelligent Four Courts man."

"In short, the sort of detective who, through hypertrophated zeal and atrophied brains, might be expected to make just the blunder I expect to make – to arrest the wrong man, search him and let him go, with a sulky apology, eh?"

"You think you can succeed in this risky plan?"

"If I were at home, in England, I should have no doubt whatsoever about it. But here your police methods are so utterly different. I'm constantly running my head into some blind wall caused by the difference in police regulations between the two countries. But this time I've planned it all out pretty carefully and I can't see how I can fail."

"How are you going to find him? By going to his home?"

"No. That's unsafe. I've thought of a far better plan. But I would rather not explain it just yet. If you and Gresham will meet me in the café here at half after six tonight, I will report progress. I've already asked Gresham to be here then. I asked him when I got the bogus warrant from him."

"It's a wonder Gresham ever helped you out by getting a false warrant. He wouldn't do such a thing for any other man on earth. But you've got him hypnotized."

They both laughed and issued from the lobby into Broadway.

A violet vender pressed forward offering his wares. The Englishman tossed a half dollar into the lad's flower tray and passed on.

"Indiscriminate charity," observed Beckwith in mock reproof.

"Not exactly. The boy seems to be trying to live honestly and to get rid of the faint of the reformatory. Besides, his mother takes a lot of pride in him. She's a real, sober, industrious woman, expert with her needle, although left-handed, and ..."

"Oh, they're protégés of yours? I didn't know ..."

"On the contrary. I never saw the boy until now."

"But the reformatory, and his industrious mother, who takes such pride in his appearance, and all that ..."

"Merely deduction. At his first step, I saw that he had the prison walk. He is too young to have been in prison; hence the reformatory. He is working – and with an evident interest in his work. His clothes are neatly mended by an experienced needlewoman. What expert needlewoman would take such wonderful care of a poor boy's clothes but his mother? And, at that, a good mother, who cared for her boy? There is all the 'mystery.'"

"But you said the mother was left-handed ..."

"When one is left-handed, she sews from left to right instead of from right to left. A glance at the patches on that lad's elbows told me the seamstress was left-handed. It's all so absurdly simple," went on The Englishman, checking the other's words of praise.

"It comes from cultivating the very common faculty of observation. I only wish I could find some such means of

deciphering the Ballard matter. I told you I formed a theory of the crime based on just such observation; but I have had no chance to amplify it or connect the stray strands, thanks to my inability to examine Craddock's rooms. Besides, there is no use in pursuing an improbable theory when one so much more likely lies just within my reach. I must leave you here. Goodbye until 6:30."

They had reached Olive Street. The Englishman walked on alone, up the latter thoroughfare, toward the post office.

At almost the same moment, Royce Ballard re-read for the third time a telegram he had received a half-hour earlier. It ran:

> "Called suddenly to Washington. Meet me at
> Union Station 3:45; important
>
> Bona Pittani"

Royce was of two minds, whether or not to obey the summons. But the conversation he had had with the young Italian artist the previous evening, coupled with his prior experience with her character at length decided him to keep the appointment. With ill grace, he started on his journey.

Reaching the Eads Bridge, Ballard passed hurriedly toward the car, looking neither to right nor to left. He, therefore, did not observe a grizzled, square-jawed man in plain clothes who had been sandwiched between a woman with a squalling baby and an Italian with a huge bundle. The square-jawed man followed Ballard.

"This is the safest way," thought The Englishman, as with black face, he leaned back puffing at his pipe and eyeing furtively the well-dressed man at the opposite end of the car.

"If I arrest him across the river, on the Illinois side, he can't summon any friend in a hurry to identify him, and the station

house to which I take him for the searching process will be too far away from his home to permit any interruption before I learn what it is he guards so carefully in his breast pocket. I really think this isn't a bad stroke."

Arrived at East St. Louis, The Englishman carefully knocked the ashes from his pipe, pocketed that redolent treasure, and leisurely followed Royce from the car.

Ballard made a tour of the relay waiting rooms, compared his watch with the two big clocks that hang at either end of the great terminal, frowned, and took to pacing impatiently up and down. On his second tour of the room, a man stepped quietly up to him and laid a hand on his shoulder. Royce turned quickly.

"Oh, you've come at last!" he began, then paused as, instead of the tall, dark girl he had expected, he confronted a grizzled, plainly-dressed man with quiet, stern eyes and square jaw.

For a fraction of a second it seemed to Royce that somewhere before, at some time, he had seen those grave, critical eyes. But the idea passed. The man was evidently a total stranger to him.

"Who the deuce are you?" he growled. "Take your hand off my shoulder. What do you want?"

"I want you, friend," said the other gruffly. "We've been looking for you for quite a while."

Ballard's face went sallow, but with a quick effort, he recovered himself.

"What do you mean?" he queried, sharply.

"Cap'n wants to see you," replied The Englishman in his best imitation of American detective methods, so far as he had been able to observe them.

Ballard made a sudden movement toward his breast pocket. The Englishman well knew the object was to conceal or destroy something he carried there, but he preferred to affect the belief that it was a weapon the other sought.

"Drop it," he said, savagely catching Royce's wrist and thrusting it downward from the region of the pocket. Then he added, more quietly:

"There are a lot of people passing. You don't want a scene. Come quietly."

For an instant, Ballard looked at him irresolutely. "You're a detective, I suppose," he said at last. "What am I charged with?"

"The captain'll tell you all that," replied The Englishman. "Come along."

"What's up?" asked a voice from behind them. Both men turned to face a policeman.

"Ah, const- officer," remarked The Englishman. "Just help me to the station house with this fellow, will you? He's ugly."

"What's he done?" asked the bluecoat. "Warrant case, I s'pose?"

"Yes," answered The Englishman glibly. "I've got a warrant."

"I don't know your face," went on the policeman. "I thought I knew all the tecs. You must be a new man."

"I am. Come, don't let's waste any more time."

"Officer," began Ballard.

"Shut up," rejoined the bluecoat courteously. "You'll have plenty of time to talk at headquarters. What's he done?" he added to The Englishman, as the trio moved toward the exit.

For an answer, The Englishman handed him the warrant. He did not wish Ballard to know the nature of the alleged charge or to lose his present state of semi-paralyzed mystification.

The officer glanced over the document and then looked at The Englishman with an incredulity that rapidly merged into suspicion.

"What's up?" thought The Englishman. "He surely can't have sense enough to know the thing's a forgery. The form and signature on the warrant are regular enough. But there's a break somewhere."

The policeman had dropped his hold on Royce Ballard's arm and now edged a step nearer The Englishman. Clearly, there was trouble ahead.

CHAPTER VI

THE HUNTER HUNTED

The Englishman, hiding under an air of impatience his growing nervousness, stood and commanded, "Come! What are we waiting for? Let us move on. I want to get this man to the station house."

For an answer, the policeman pocketed the warrant.

"Give that back to me," commanded The Englishman sharply. "What on earth is the matter?" he wondered uneasily.

"This warrant," began the policeman.

"Well," interrupted The Englishman. "It's regular and correct, isn't it?"

"All reg'lar and c'rect," assented the policeman. "The only thing the matter with it is that it's a Missouri warrant and you're servin' it in Illinois."

"Well," said The Englishman again.

"Well," echoed the bluecoat. "How long have you been on the force not to know that Missouri warrant don't cut no ice over in Illinois? You're a nice sort of 'tec,' ain't you? Say," he added suspiciously as The Englishman reddened with anger under the

knowledge of the error he had made. "There ain't a cop or a detective in this whole country that don't know that a warrant's only good for the state it's made out in. I believe you're no more a detective than I am. What's your game?"

As he spoke, he threw back the lapel of The Englishman's coat.

"Just as I thought," he exclaimed. "Not even a badge. I don't know just what your game is, but I'll take you to the station house all right. And this feller you were bluffin' 'll go along as a witness."

The Englishman, seeing that he had made too grave an error to permit his continuance of the role of Four Courts man, tried a new tack.

"Look here, officer," he whispered. "This is just a joke of mine. Help me out on it and it's a $10 in your ..."

"Cut it out!" ordered the policeman tersely. "The capt'n at our station's a fine judge of jokes. We'll just put it up to him."

Catching The Englishman and Royce Ballard each by an arm, he started down the steps.

The Englishman walked meekly along, offering no resistance or remonstrance. Never before in all his varied experience had he been confronted with a dilemma like this. Many a time had his life been in danger, but never once had a mere policeman overmatched him. He felt for the moment almost helpless against this mere nonentity whose brain was immeasurably inferior to his own.

"It is my own folly," he thought wrathfully. "But for my conceit in wanting to crow over Beckwith and Gresham, I'd have told them this plan of mine and they'd have explained this warrant business to me. In England, a warrant made out at Scotland Yard is effective in every corner of the British Isles. How was I to know that these

Yankees restrict the power of a warrant to the mere state in which it happens to be issued? But what a godsend the ferries must be to criminals. In England, we'd frame a law in a hurry that would shut off such a splendid path of escape from them. It's as hard to catch a St. Louis crook who crosses to Illinois as to get a London refugee who escapes to France. But unless I do something quickly, my hopes of discovering the Ballard murderer are at an end, and my name will become the laughingstock of two continents."

Like most geniuses, The Englishman was particularly sensitive to ridicule. This latter fear, therefore, awakened the keenest faculties of self-preservation.

The policeman and his double convoy had well-nigh reached the bottom of the long flight of steps. Whatever was to be done by The Englishman must be done at once.

The policeman was walking between the two, The Englishman being on his right. As the latter had shown no signs of flight, the bluecoat was not expecting trouble. Suddenly, on the fourth step from the bottom, The Englishman's foot apparently slipped. He plunged awkwardly forward and, owing to the grasp of the officer on his left arm, swung sharply to the left.

The sharp tug had pulled both Ballard and the policeman forward, and owing to the direction The Englishman's body had taken, one of his long legs was thrust across the third step directly in front of his two companions. Against this barrier, they stumbled before either could recover from the forward impetus which The Englishman's sudden misstep had caused.

The trio fell in a profane, awkward, tangled heap at the foot of the stairs.

The Englishman, being uppermost, was first to extricate himself. He delayed only long enough to snatch the bogus warrant

from the policeman and thrust it into his own pocket. But the delay was well-nigh fatal to his plan of escape. For the agile bluecoat was on his feet in a trice and sprang on his prisoner. Quick as he was, The Englishman was quicker. A left-hander in the mouth sent the policeman back against the wall. He recovered himself at once, but not before The Englishman had dashed through the idle crowd that had begun to collect, and passed through the entrance out into the street.

His pursuer was scarcely a yard behind him, and a second policeman joined in the chase, as did a half dozen bystanders.

Across the street, dodging in and out among bridge vehicles and trolley cars, The Englishman fled, his foes close on his heels.

It was his first visit to East St. Louis. In a strange land, he was trying to escape from men whose home ground it was. Another fugitive would have fled aimlessly, would have tried to double, and would most infallibly, have been caught in short order. The Englishman, on the contrary, ran straight for the car stables diagonally opposite. Rushing just ahead of his pursuers into the shed and slipping between two cars, he made for one of the low doors leading to the rear of the building. Slamming this door almost in the face of his foremost pursuer, he shot the bolt.

Barely five seconds passed before the combined shoulders of the two policemen had smashed the door in. But that brief interval was apparently sufficient. For, search as they would, no sign of The Englishman could they find.

A large crowd had by this time gathered in front of the car stables, and the baffled officers were treated to a good amount of guying.

"Where's your other prisoner?" inquired an old countryman. "The nice-dressed one you was holding when the other feller took it into his head to scoot?"

The first policeman started angrily. In the pursuit of The Englishman and the hopes of promotion for so clever a capture, he had quite forgotten Royce Ballard. The latter had taken advantage of this forgetfulness to move away unobserved and board a bridge car.

"Guess the pair of 'em was too slick for ya, eh?" jeered the countryman.

"Move on, now," threatened the policeman, cholerically, "before I run you in too."

"Fore you run me in instead. I guess you mean constable," chuckled the old man, encouraged by the grins of the crowd. "I ain't seen ya running ennybody in so far."

The policeman treated his rural tormentor to a disgusted glare.

"Guess you're the funny man at the village store up to Mitchell or some such place?" he sneered. "Chase back there; you're too witty to be loose in town."

Instead of following this advice, the old countryman slouched across to the ferry house, bought a ticket to St. Louis, and sighed contentedly as he found a vacant seat in a car.

"That was a pretty close call. After this, I'll study up some of this queer country's criminal laws before I play detective again. Just the same," he added doggedly, "I'll find what Royce Ballard carried so carefully in his breast pocket. One scheme has failed. The next shall succeed."

CHAPTER VII

A NEW PLAN

G resham and Beckwith sat smoking and taking desultory drinks from long glasses at a table beside a pillar in the Planters' Café.

"What's happened to The Englishman, I wonder?" observed Beckwith for the tenth time. "He promised to be here by 6:30. It's nearly 7."

"When he does come," said Gresham, "you may be sure he'll bring with him what he went for. That fellow simply can't lose. I'll bet $10 even that he got away with the goods, made the arrest, had Ballard searched, found what he wanted, and cleared out."

"I'll take that bet," announced Beckwith, after a moment's reflection. "I've no doubt you'll win, but a wager will help change the tedium of waiting into something like suspense. You should have seen his makeup. It was great. He'll probably have it on when he comes here."

"I wish you'd lay your cards on the table," growled Gresham fretfully.

"What do you mean?"

"Why, you know, whether this Englishman is really Sherlock Holmes or if he is the original from which the character of Sherlock

Holmes was drawn. If he is really Sherlock Holmes, why should he be so stubborn as to refuse to say so? If he isn't, what could possibly be his game in letting me believe that he is?"

"I'm afraid I can't help you out," said Beckwith.

"I ..."

"Then I stick to my belief that he is really Sherlock Holmes and that he hides his identity in order to avoid notoriety. Isn't that so?"

"In his own good time he'll doubtless explain everything clearly. In the meantime, I suppose I must keep on calling him 'The Englishman,' and – hello, here he comes."

The Englishman, not the squared-jawed Four Courts man nor the elderly rustic, sauntered in, nodded curtly to the two and sat down.

Beckwith saw at a glance that something was amiss – something serious enough to ruffle the gigantic composure of even a man of The Englishman's self-control.

Gresham, denser and less tactful, asked: "What luck, old man?"

"None," snapped The Englishman. "Get me a Scotch highball, waiter."

"None?" echoed Gresham, amazed. "No luck at all? I thought you never failed."

"Did you?" observed The Englishman coldly. "Well, you know better now."

"Didn't even ..."

"Oh, don't rub it in, Gresham," interposed Beckwith. "He'll tell us about it in his own time. If he missed seeing Ballard today, he'll catch him by the same trick tomorrow."

"I saw him," said The Englishman, somewhat less reluctantly and speaking fast as though to be quit of some unpleasant duty.

"I saw him at a place to which I had induced him to come. I served the warrant and ..."

"Where was this place?" interrupted Gresham.

"Relay Station."

"East St. Louis!" cried both detectives in surprise.

The Englishman nodded.

"Why, man," exclaimed Gresham, "a Missouri warrant is no ..."

"No use in Illinois," finished The Englishman.

"Yes, my friend, I know that quite well. In fact, the knowledge has been pretty thoroughly instilled into me this afternoon. It comes late, but it's very effective now that I've acquired it. I'm not likely to forget. If I'd known a bit earlier ..."

"But," suggested Beckwith, "why didn't you tell us where you were going to meet him? We could ..."

"Because I was a fool, I suppose," replied The Englishman.

"Think of the greatest detective on earth talking like that!" muttered Gresham, dumbfounded at the downfall of his hero.

"Now ..."

Beckwith kicked him furtively and the Four Courts man subsided.

The Englishman recounted tersely, yet vividly, his experience of the afternoon. As he did so, the gloomy disgust on Gresham's face gradually cleared away, and, as The Englishman reached the point in the recital where he described the way in which, as the pseudo countryman, he had joked the baffled bluecoat, the old look of admiration redawned in Gresham's eyes.

"Gee!" he cried. "You're great, all right, even if you are a little shy on interstate criminal law. And, now, what are you going to do?"

"Do? I'm going to do what I set out to. To get this precious packet or whatever it is that Royce Ballard carries in his breast pocket. The thing that Bona Pittani hinted contained the secret of Cyril Ballard's murder."

"But that warrant trick won't work twice. The man 'll be on his guard."

"Of course he will. This time I'll take no chances of falling foul of your queer Yankee criminal laws. My experience has been that though laws differ in every country, criminals of all nations are practically the same. Good! Then I'll be a criminal, a highwayman, a hold-up as you American call it. I intend to hold up Mr. Royce Ballard and rob him of this treasure."

"In Illinois," laughed Beckwith.

"No, on Fourth Street, St. Louis."

"Fourth Street! Why Fourth Street's in the busiest section of the city. It's crowded. What are you thinking of?"

"I admit it is crowded in the daytime and I have no intention of luring Ballard into a crowd and asking him to stand and deliver. There are two places on earth which are, to me, the acme of

deserted desolation. One is the center of the Sahara. The other is a downtown St. Louis street after business hours."

"Oh, you mean to get him to Fourth Street at night and hold him up? But won't he be a little coy about taking the bait after a lesson like this afternoon's? He ..."

"You people might give me credit for a little intelligence in spite of my blunder today," complained The Englishman. "Kindly listen to the outline of my plans and see if it strikes you as foolish. It is daring, I admit. But, with a little skill, there is no reason why it should not succeed."

"We're listening," said Gresham, more respectfully.

"I've had my eye on Mr. Royce Ballard for some time. In a Fourth Street office building, less than a block east of Broadway, he has hired a room which he has fitted up as a laboratory."

"Laboratory? I remember chemistry was the one study he cared for at the medical school. That's where he made these poison tablets and ..."

"Yes, if he made them and if they were poison. He keeps the laboratory locked. Even the janitor can't get in. He hires the room under a false name. He goes there two or three afternoons a week and stays (presumably working on his experiments) sometimes until 10 or 11 o'clock at night. I've been watching him, you see."

"But how can you tell when he is to be there?"

"He is most scrupulous in the matter of dress.

"On the afternoon he is going to his laboratory, he doesn't get into a frock coat and topper, but wears business clothes. To attract less attention in the business district, I fancy. Well, his valet has undertaken to send me a telegram, on the quiet, the next afternoon

he wears a business suit. I shall be waiting for him at the door of his office, taking care there is no policeman near. The rest should be easy."

"Do you know," remarked Beckwith, "there is something utterly uncanny and unnatural about all this case. First, Cyril Ballard's sudden death, the moment of darkness, and the chord of music from the piano. Then this mysterious 'something' that Royce Ballard carries always in his breast pocket which connects him with the crime. What can it be? Then the fact that no trace of any known poison was found in Cyril's body. It baffles me."

"We're listening," said Gresham, more respectfully.

"The key of it all seems to be the packet, whatever it is, that Royce guards so zealously," said The Englishman, "unless ..."

"Still thinking of that improbable first theory of yours which you refuse to tell us?" asked Beckwith as The Englishman paused.

"Yes, but that is all so improbable. I'll send you men word the day I am to try my hold-up experiment on Mr. Royce Ballard. Then you can come to my rooms and wait there for my report until I return, if you like, and hear my report. I think I can promise you that I won't return empty-handed again."

The Englishman had not greatly exaggerated when he had described the downtown business district of St. Louis as the most desolate spot on earth after business hours. And so it appeared to him as he strolled southward along lower Broadway on the night following his East St. Louis experience.

The streets leading to the bridge still contained a few hurrying figures. Broadway, so thronged in daylight hours, was nearly empty; the nearly vacant yellow cars whizzing along at greater intervals and at far greater speed than would have been permissible before dark.

But, most of the side streets stretched away, silent, empty, and dead as the Tombs of Luxor. The tread of stray policemen or belated workers awoke weird echoes from the high, forbidding fronts of silent buildings. The electric lights seemed to intensify rather than dissipate the gloomy desolation of it all.

Turning east from Broadway, The Englishman strolled leisurely through Fourth Street. A light twinkled in a single window on the fifth floor of a building half a block down the street. There Ballard was still at work. Glancing about to see that no policeman or watchman was visible, The Englishman hurriedly tried the door leading to the upper floors. It was locked. He dared not risk exposure so early in the evening by picking the lock, so he slipped into the protecting angle of a wide first-floor sign and waited.

Hour after hour passed, and the district grew even emptier and more silent. "He's working late tonight," commented The Englishman as midnight struck from a distant bell. "It should be safe to try to break the lock now. I'd rather take my chances upstairs

alone with him in his own laboratory than in the street where a half dozen of these lynx-eyed American police may drop down on us at any moment."

He stepped forth from his hiding place.

A shrewd eye would have been needed to detect the dapper English detective or the Four Courts man or the old countryman in the grim-faced, shabbily dressed thug who stood revealed by the glow from a far-off electric light. Not so clearly a tough character as to attract notice, there was, nevertheless, an ill-groomed, unshaven, air about the man in this new disguise, which would divert any suspicion from the theory that the proposed attack was not a mere mercenary hold-up, perpetrated by a professional.

Another glance up and down the street.

"What can have happened to Ballard to keep him there so late?" muttered The Englishman, as he bent to the task of picking the lock. "He never worked so late before. Can anything be the matter?"

As he was applying an odd-shaped steel instrument to the lock he suddenly leaped back. But he was too late to escape notice. Even as The Englishman sought to retreat, the door he had been assailing was flung wide open. The Englishman braced himself for the contingency and stood his ground.

The Englishman braced himself.

CHAPTER VIII

A HOLD–UP AND WHAT FOLLOWED

A man stepped briskly out, closing the door behind him. Its spring lock clicked and both men were locked out, thus spoiling The Englishman's hope of encountering Ballard in the hall.

He would have attacked the newcomer as the door opened had he been sure that it was Royce. But, before he had clearly identified Ballard by the dim gleam of the distant electric light, the door was shut.

Ballard, surprised to be thus confronted, took an involuntary backward step which brought him against the closed door.

From this point of vantage, he scanned keenly the indistinct face and dim figure of the man before him. There seemed something vaguely familiar about the intruder.

"What do you want?" he asked very sharply.

"Could you give a poor feller the price of ..."

"No, I couldn't," he snapped, cutting short the ill-dressed man's sniveling appeal, "and I ..."

"Hands up!"

The Englishman's order was short and imperative as a pistol shot. With a quick move, he had covered Ballard with a revolver.

Royce Ballard did not number cowardice among his vices.

Neither was he slow-witted.

His antagonist was not four feet off. Royce threw up both arms obediently, but as he did so he caught The Englishman's right wrist in his own left hand, twisting his assailant's wrist so sharply that the revolver clattered to the pavement.

With a simultaneous gesture of his right hand, Royce drew a pistol from the side pocket of the sack coat he wore and thrust it into The Englishman's face.

For the tiniest interval of space, The Englishman pictured himself again returning to Gresham and Beckwith, outwitted by the man.

The thought decided him.

Scarcely was the pistol on a level with his head than he dropped to one knee, seized Ballard about the legs, and threw him backward over his head to the sidewalk.

The entire movement did not occupy half a second.

Royce Ballard, taken totally by surprise, fell heavily, the top of his head striking the pavement with such force that his stiff derby alone averted a fracture of the skull.

As it was, he lay there, huddled senseless, inert.

Another swift glance up and down the street and The Englishman was on his knees beside the prostrate man. With skilled fingers, he ransacked his victim's clothes.

Resisting his impulse first to explore the breast pockets, he drew forth Royce's watch and then a roll of bills that were in his right-hand trousers pocket. Then he turned his attention to Ballard's other pockets. Plunging his hand first into the inside breast pockets of the senseless man's coat, he drew out a number of papers and letters.

Then, continuing his search, he pulled forth a similar but smaller collection from Ballard's inner waistcoat pockets.

With skilled fingers, he ransacked his victim's clothes.

The unconscious victim began to show signs of returning life.

A hasty search assured The Englishman that the pockets were now all empty. Whatever document or packet Ballard had so carefully guarded must now be in the heap of papers in his conqueror's hands.

The Englishman's sensitive fingertips could find no trace of a secret pocket or of valuables sewn into the coat, waistcoat, or shirt.

He rose to his feet, bundling his spoils into an inner pocket of his own coat.

As he rose, he saw a policeman turn into Fourth Street from the west and advance leisurely toward them.

Ballard, too, his senses more fully returning, struggled to a sitting position, his eyes, under the battered wreck of his derby, fixed dazedly on The Englishman.

Clearly, there was no time to be lost.

The Englishman walked toward Broadway as rapidly as he dared, trusting to luck that the policeman was too far away to take in the situation.

Ballard, however, the mists clearing from his throbbing brain, had scrambled to his feet and was staggering in dizzy pursuit of the marauder.

"Help!" yelled Royce thickly, as The Englishman quickened his pace. "Help! Police!"

The policeman broke into a run and reached the injured man. Royce pointed toward the now fleeing Englishman and gasped out a few words that made clear the situation to the officer.

"Stop!" shouted the policeman, drawing his revolver and rushing along in The Englishman's wake. "Stop or I'll shoot!"

The cliff-like sides of the dead thoroughfare awoke and re-echoed to the roar of the bluecoat's .44. The pursuer, at the same time, banged on the pavement with his nightstick.

The Englishman had reached Broadway. His pursuers were a half block behind.

"If only a car will happen along now!" he panted.

Luck was with him. Less than a block away, a northbound trolley car came bowling along at almost top rate. Delayed at a crossing, the motorman was taking advantage of the deserted state of the streets, the lateness of the hour and the fact that there was no car within a mile ahead of him, to make up for lost time by a burst of speed.

The Englishman hailed the car. As there was no "next car" in sight, the motorman, for a wonder, slackened speed, grudgingly slowing up sufficiently to allow the fugitive to leap aboard. As The Englishman's feet touched the lowest step, the conductor rang the bell twice, and the car again bounded forward.

As it did so, a Broadway policeman, who had heard the raps of his colleague's nightstick and had arrived in time to see The Englishman's fleeing form, but too late to stop his boarding the car, shouted to the conductor to stop.

At the same moment, the conductor caught sight of the first policeman and Royce as they emerged into Broadway, not fifty feet away from the car.

A glance at the panting, ill-clad figure on the platform beside him was enough for the Transit employee. With one hand he jerked the bell violently. With the other, he collared The Englishman. The car slowed down with a jar and Royce and the two policemen, sighting The Englishman, bounded toward their prey.

Other pedestrians, springing up as if by magic from the seemingly vacant thoroughfare, joined in the rush.

The Englishman was in perhaps the tightest fix of his career.

What chance, he wondered, would he, as a foreigner, stand in court when it should be proved that he had held up and robbed a respectable St. Louisan?

A wild idea of rushing through the car, leaping off the front platform, and taking his chances in flight flashed through his mind. But he dismissed it as he heard the answering raps of nightsticks further up the street and saw how completely his escape was cut off.

For better or worse, his resolve was taken within a fraction of a moment from the time the conductor had seized him and signaled for the car to stop.

With his left hand, he snatched off the conductor's cap. With his clenched right, he landed heavily on the conductor's throat. The man toppled backward, missed the top step, and fell sprawling in the mud of the street.

Before the conductor touched the ground, before the foremost of the pursuers could lay hand on the platform rail, before the car had come to a stop, The Englishman jerked the bell twice. With a lurch and a heave, the car sprang forward.

The motorman had heard the disturbance but had been unable, from his post, in that instant's interval, to determine the cause. Least of all did he suspect that his colleague was in trouble. If there had been a row of any sort, he thought, the conductor would come through and tell him. In the meantime, he heralded with delight the order to start. For they were late, and lateness meant the loss of pay and sleep.

The foremost policeman (he who had discovered Royce's plight) sprinted, seized the rear rail, and swung himself to the lowest step of the platform. Before he could fairly balance himself, a well-directed kick in the chest sent him spinning into the street.

The Englishman carefully took off his own derby, substituted the conductor's cap for it, and stood stiffly on the rear platform in conventional attitude. No one seeing the car in that deceptive light could have guessed there was anything amiss with its crew.

The pursuers were quickly distanced, and a policeman from further up the street howled to the motorman to stop and attempted to leap aboard the flying car. But at the first touch of the motorman's hand to the brake, that decisive double ring sounded again, and the bluecoat was left far astern.

The motorman stared back through the car. There were no passengers, and there on the back platform, dimly seen behind the glass of the door, the conductor was standing unconcerned. There was no time to stop and ask questions, yet the motorman wondered peevishly why his partner did not come forward and explain.

"If only no truck coming from a cross street stops us, we are safe for the moment," sighed The Englishman in relief.

Then a second, less welcome thought struck him. Though they had outdistanced all pursuit, yet it was probable – nay, certain – that the uptown police would be telephoned and would head them off. And, moreover, the present gratifying rate of speed must cease as soon as the car overhauled the one ahead of it.

It seemed that he was by no means out of the woods. The gravest dangers were yet to come – perils that were to call for all his vast fund of cleverness and resources.

CHAPTER IX

A TROLLEY CAR RACE

H ere was a dilemma. For the moment, The Englishman was comparatively safe.

His ruse of capturing the car, finding it devoid of passengers, and securing the motorman's cooperation – a cooperation as hearty as it was totally unconscious – had enabled him to leave his pursuers far in the rear.

He half smiled as he pictured the furious, profane group – the policemen, the muddy conductor, Royce Ballard, and the chance pedestrians – toiling along on foot in pursuit of a trolley car that was going at the rate of almost 26 miles an hour.

But the danger ahead was nonetheless grave.

The policemen had doubtless telephoned uptown to have the car stopped. Officers were probably already waiting somewhere along the track in front.

Then, too, The Englishman's car was rapidly gaining on the car in front of it. Long before North Market Street could be reached, they must perforce slacken speed, even supposing that no vehicle from a side street should sooner obstruct rapid progress.

At Grand Avenue, at the furthest, police must stop them.

Carr Street was already passed, the car almost grazing the noses of a pair of horses drawing a wagon.

Chancing to glance backward toward the driver, whose scintillant profanity was still splitting the night, The Englishman's gaze became fixed and rigid.

Distant, but whizzing forward at top speed, a northbound trolley car was dashing along in their wake. With eyes phenomenally far-sighted by nature, and whose keenness had been further trained by a lifetime of observation, The Englishman could see in the lighted interior of the pursuing car three bluecoated policemen. He understood the whole situation at once.

His pursuers had taken a leaf out of his own book and seized and impressed into service the first trolley car that had followed the one taken by The Englishman and were ordering the motorman 'in the name of the law' to crowd on all power in the hope of overhauling their prey.

The Englishman was thus menaced fore and aft. At any moment now, the chase might end.

A belated pedestrian hailed him at this moment.

"Take the next car," shouted the pseudo-conductor, with a grim smile at his own jest, and the chase continued.

A look at the next illuminated corner as it flashed by showed the fugitive he had reached Mullanphy Street. The pursuers were still too far distant for the average eye to detect The Englishman's figure on the rear platform of the car they were chasing. But probably, through some lingering reluctance on the part of The Englishman's motorman to risk his car's mechanism by a too-excessive fracture of the speed ordinances, the second car was gradually creeping closer.

On whirled the mad race between black and silent walls, rows of dark windows gazing down the sightless eyes on the sport.

The street, which by daylight forms the pulsating plethoric chief artery of traffic for one of the greatest cities on earth, slept silent, inert, almost disserted at this late hour.

"The next street's Angelica," thought The Englishman nervously. "There's no more time to be wasted."

He pulled the bell. Reluctantly the motorman applied the brakes.

The portion of the block where they now were was comparatively dark. As the speed slackened, The Englishman jerked the bell twice and, as he did so, he tossed the borrowed cap to the platform, resumed his own hat, and sprang lightly to the ground. The motorman put on speed once more and the conductorless car sped on up Broadway.

As the second car rushed on a half minute later, a man strolling unsteadily into Broadway from the eastern part of Angelica Street paused in a drunken wonder to watch the unusual speed, and incidentally to take note of its passengers. These consisted of three policemen, one of them covered with mud; an extra conductor, hatless and similarly disfigured; and a well-dressed man holding a smashed derby.

As the car passed, the drunken pedestrian recovered his sobriety and, with marvelous suddenness, crossed Broadway, and walked rapidly up Angelica Street. Arrived at the Bellefontaine line, he took a car south.

"I wonder if it's worthwhile waiting any longer for The Englishman?" remarked Gresham, yawning and noisily snapping the

case of his big watch. "When he tipped us off that this was the night and said we might wait here in his rooms till he got back from holding up Ballard, I expected he'd be back by about 11. It's nearly 1."

"I, for one, shall wait," answered Beckwith.

"It'll be worth waiting for."

"You think he'll get what he went for this time?"

"I know it," said Beckwith calmly. "Want to get back that $10 by betting on it?"

"You're on."

"What makes you so confident?"

"Any man may fail once. But that Englishman isn't the man to give an encore performance of a failure. He'll go through Royce Ballard's clothes this time or he'll never come back alive."

"Want to get back that $10 by betting on it?"

"Never come back alive?" echoed a voice from the door. "That's a rather doleful prophecy, old man."

"The Englishman!" exclaimed the two detectives.

"What luck?" asked Gresham.

For reply, The Englishman pulled from various pockets a watch, a roll of bills, and a handful of papers, all of which he laid on the table.

Gresham solemnly produced two $5 bills and handed them over to Beckwith. The Englishman smiled as he noted the transfer.

"So this time it was Beckwith who had the faith, eh?" he observed.

Gresham laughed sheepishly. "I might have known better," he said. "Beckwith said you couldn't fail twice. Now let's have a look at your booty."

The Englishman was sorting out the money and jewelry from the papers.

"Went through him pretty thoroughly, didn't you?" commented Gresham, viewing the treasure approvingly, "but what are you going to do with the cash and the watch?"

"I just brought them along to avert Ballard's suspicion from my real object," replied The Englishman. "I'm going to put them up in a neat little package and send them back to Ballard with a note to the effect that I am the 'gentleman burglar,' Raffles, whose antics have been exploited in the papers of late. I'll tell him I stole his valuables just for amusement and that I herewith return them intact. The papers will have another pretty Raffles mystery to amuse them."

"How the real 'gentleman burglar,' whoever he is, will swear when he reads about it," chuckled Beckwith, appreciatively.

"Gentleman burglar!" sneered Gresham. "Lord! How I hate that term. It would be as sensible to speak of an 'honest shoplifter,' or a 'black-haired albino.' Whenever a thief doesn't murder his victim or burn down the house or eat one of the children, he's heralded as a 'gentleman burglar.' Say, let's get at those papers, now."

Deftly, swiftly, with speed born of long experience, the trio attacked the little pile of papers among which, they believed, lurked the key to the Ballard murder mystery.

"It's probably the chemical formula for the poison in the tablets," hazarded Gresham.

But no such formula came to light. Letters, bills, memoranda – those were all the searchers could find. No chemical formula, no cipher, no cryptogram or other incriminating document came to light.

The letters, which Gresham unsurreptitiously proceeded to read, had no direct bearing on the murder.

"It's as I feared," sighed The Englishman at last, leaning back in his chair and lighting another cigarette. "The fellow took fright yesterday and he's chosen some other hiding place for his treasure. We're sold!"

"This sounds interesting," said Gresham, looking up from one of the letters he was reading.

"What is it?" asked The Englishman.

"The signature's torn off. But the letter means something. Listen:

"Dear Mr. Ballard,

> *Many thanks for the tablets. You are sure they are just what I want? Swift, certain, and painless? Remember I cannot afford to take the risk of any mistake. Since your brother will not ..."*

"That's all there is. Signature's torn off."

"No date at the top?"

"Yes. March 3."

"The very morning before Cyril Ballard was killed!" cried Beckwith.

The Englishman had already snatched the mutilated note from Gresham's hand and was scanning it eagerly through his pocket microscope.

"Paper of German make," he muttered, thinking aloud.

"Writer a German of artistic temperament. Gentle by nature, but capable of sudden anger if slighted or wronged. Highly sensitive. Abnormally developed muscles in the forearm and hand. Pianist probably. Professional. Wait," scanning a thumbmark so faint as to be invisible to the naked eye, "writer about 5 feet 11 inches tall, slender, and over 30. And here's the mark of Royce Ballard's fingers on the corner of the sheet. He ..."

Beckwith came around the table and glanced over The Englishman's shoulder at the careless, scrawling chirography.

"Siurd Von Rickerl!" he exclaimed. "I know his handwriting well!"

"Von Rickerl!" said Gresham, amazed. "The young piano genius that's engaged to Miss Durant?"

"And it was at the musicale in his honor at Craddock's that Cyril Ballard was killed," went on Beckwith. "You remember, he had just gone into the alcove where the piano was, when Cyril ran in ahead of him and seated himself at the piano. For an instant, the two were alone in the alcove, the portières cutting them off from the view of the rest of the guests. Then Von Rickerl came out alone. Cyril struck one chord on the piano, then fell back dead. It looks bad. If ..."

"But Von Rickerl testified later that during the instant he was in the alcove he saw another man standing there beside the piano," put in Gresham.

"That looks still worse," answered Beckwith. "If he really killed Cyril Ballard, it would sidetrack suspicion from him if it were thought another man was there too. I know he always disliked Cyril Ballard – most of us did, for that matter – and after he 'shook' the Pittani girl I hear he made violent love to Iris Durand. There's a motive straightaway for the killing. But Van Rickerl's the last man on earth whom I'd suspect of such an act."

"What I can't understand," observed Gresham, "is how any man who planned to poison another could have been fool enough to write such an incriminating letter as that."

"A professional crook wouldn't" replied Beckwith.

"It shows how little sense and forethought Von Rickerl took."

"This letter alone," interrupted Gresham, "should be enough evidence for arresting Von Rickerl for the murder and Royce Ballard as an accessory. But ..."

"But," cut in The Englishman, speaking for the first time since the discussion had begun. "But I've had another lesson in the mistakes a man may make in this country of yours. I'd have sworn that Von Rickerl could not commit a premeditated murder. A sudden stabbing, perhaps, but ..."

"It seems to me," said Beckwith, "that our real work is just beginning. Unless I'm much mistaken, there is something exciting in store."

CHAPTER X

ON THE TRAIL ONCE MORE

As they rose to go, The Englishman said to his visitors, "There is something else to be taken into account. And it brings me back in a measure to my first improbable theory, which I shall explain to you in due time.

"I've told you I was waiting until I could receive certain chemicals from my own laboratory in London before I could determine whether or not the tablets found in Cyril's pepsin vial really held some subtle poison that had refused to respond to the regular medical tests. Well, those chemicals arrived this morning. I spent most of the day making tests on the tablets and on specimens of the viscera. I've been so much absorbed in the adventure I had tonight that I forgot to tell you earlier about the experiments I made."

"Did you find what the tablets were made of?"

"Yes. They were composed of a strong precipitate of thalesia silicate. Thalesia, as you may know, is one of the deadliest, swiftest vegetable drugs known to the Malays. Its traces are not discernible through ordinary tests. Royce Ballard's knowledge of chemistry must have been above the ordinary if he could produce and use that stuff. But ..."

"But what?"

"But Cyril Ballard was not poisoned."

"Not poisoned? Why, I thought you said ..."

"The tablets which were mixed with his pepsin tablets were deadly poison. But it chanced that he took none of them."

"How do you know?"

"By my examination of the viscera. There are no traces of thalesia poisoning found there.

"I used an infallible test, but nothing appeared."

"Then how did Cyril Ballard die?"

"I am almost inclined to agree with the coroner's physician – that the man was frightened to death."

"But how? In a crowded room like that, and all in an instant, too? Besides, he had nerves like iron."

"He either died of fright," affirmed The Englishman doggedly, "or else from the only other cause that could produce the same effect on the face and body."

"What cause is that?"

"Death by a stroke of lightning."

Beckwith and Gresham laughed.

"Lightning? In midwinter and on a perfectly clear night?" exclaimed Beckwith. "I think we can dispense with the lightning theory. Even the idea that he died of fright seems less ridiculous than that."

The Englishman shrugged his shoulders.

Gresham asked: "If you'd already found out that Cyril Ballard didn't die by poison, why did you run his brother down tonight?"

"Because I thought the secret of Cyril's real mode of death might be about him, for one thing. For another, I was convinced he had intended to poison his brother, even if he did not succeed in doing so. And I wanted proof of it. I've almost enough now to work on."

"But it seems to me we are as far off as ever as to the real murderer and the manner of the murder."

"Does it?" asked The Englishman with a smile.

"On the contrary, I am already on a new trail. And this time I shall win."

"I don't know your game," observed Gresham as he arose to go, "but I am backing you."

In the fire-lit library of Iris Durand's home sat a man and a girl. It was late in the afternoon of the day following The Englishman's adventure with Royce Ballard.

"The papers all had accounts of it this morning," Siurd Von Rickerl was saying. "The thief actually escaped on a cable car."

"But didn't Mr. Ballard recognize him?"

"No, I believe not. But he is terribly cut up over the whole affair. It seems he has some sort of idea that he is being dogged for some mysterious purpose, and it's gotten on his nerves. To make matters more inexplicable, this morning he received a package, by

messenger, containing all the stolen articles, together with a note signed 'Raffles.'"

"How queer!"

"Queer? Everything is queer lately. The death of Cyril Ballard, this robbery, and all. Thank heaven, Liebchen, we shall be married, you and I, in a few weeks and go to my own dear country, where things are natural, and where freaks and tragedies are the exceptions and not the rule, as in this crazy America of yours. My fortunes may not be as bright financially over there, but life will be more peaceful!"

"It has been such a long wait," sighed Iris, "and now that fame and wealth have at last come to you, I can hardly realize that the weary delay is over."

"Yes," answered Siurd, bending tenderly over her white hand. "Nothing can check our plans now. Nothing except ..."

"Dr. Watts!" announced a servant.

The lovers started; Von Rickerl with impatience at the breaking up of the tête-à-tête, Iris Durand in surprise that a man whom she had scarcely met three times in her life should presume to call on her.

The Englishman entered the room, reading at a glance both emotions.

"I am afraid I intrude," he said, gently, as Iris came forward to greet him, "but believe me, the intrusion is necessary. Ah, Herr Von Rickerl, I hoped to find you here. I am fortunate."

Iris's surprise at his visit gave place to greater amazement at the change in the visitor's manner. Heretofore he had always appeared to her a silent, stupid man, with somewhat lackluster eyes and a

drooping jaw. Today his eye was keen, his jaw set, and his voice and bearing those of alertness and high intelligence.

"I called," resumed The Englishman, "because I had some questions to ask. Questions the immediate solution of which will save future annoyance to you both."

"But, Dr. Watt ..." began Iris.

"Pardon me," interposed The Englishman. "I have taken the liberty of studying St. Louis incognito. May I, in confidence, lay aside the incognito for a few moments and resume my own name?" and he mentioned that name. "My friend, Mr. Beckwith, whom I asked to join me here, will vouch for me. Have I your permission, Herr Von Rickerl, to ask them?"

"Certainly," answered the mystified German, "but ..."

"They deal with the Ballard murder," continued The Englishman, apparently engaged in smoothing out his gloves, yet never ceasing to scrutinize Von Rickerl's face.

"The Ballard murder?" echoed Siurd, puzzled.

"Yes. You were there, I think, when Ballard died."

"I was. I stood within a few feet of him," replied Siurd with a slight shudder.

"You saw another man, I think, in the alcove where the piano stood. Can you describe him?"

"No. I did not notice him especially, nor remember until afterward that he was there. All I know is that he was in evening dress, like the rest of us."

"You were not well that evening?" said The Englishman, suddenly. "What was the matter?"

Siurd glanced up in surprise.

"Who told you?" he said. "Yes, I was not well. I had been working too hard and my nerves were shaky."

"You had not seen a doctor, I believe."

"No. I do not like doctors. A friend, an acquaintance, at least ..."

"An acquaintance named Royce Ballard, who dabbles in chemistry and medicine," interposed The Englishman, "told you of some sort of tonic that was good for bracing the nerves and sent you some. And you wrote, thanking him, I think, and asking him if the medicine was swift, sure and ..."

"How – how do you know all that?" gasped Von Rickerl; "he promised me he would not mention it. I wanted the tonic to get me into condition for my concert at the Odeon the next afternoon, but he promised me ..."

"Oh, he kept his promise as far as I know," said The Englishman. "He didn't tell me. I merely deduced it."

"You can deduce life stories," began Von Rickerl, curiously. Then ..."

"Oh, not always. But it will not take a genius to deduce a perfectly happy life story for Herr Von Rickerl," said The Englishman, gayly, with a glance toward Miss Durand.

"Thank you for answering my questions. They have told me what I already believed. I am nonetheless glad to have my belief confirmed."

As he descended the steps of the Durand house, he met Beckwith.

"Come," he suggested, linking his arm in the latter's.

"Let's go around to Royce Ballard's rooms. Gresham will meet us at the door. I've found out all I wanted to know about Von Rickerl. He's as innocent of the murder as the sweet-faced sweetheart of his.

"The time has come to spring the trap on Royce. He didn't kill his brother, for Cyril didn't take the tablets Royce put into his pepsin bottle. But Royce doesn't know that. He still thinks he's Cyril's murderer. And what's more, Bona Pittani thinks so."

Arrived at the bachelor apartment house on Grand Avenue where Royce Ballard's rooms were, they found Gresham awaiting them.

"He's in, all right," remarked Gresham with a grin.

"Shall we go up? I've bribed his servant to admit us."

"What's the joke?" asked Beckwith as the grin still played about the detective's face.

"Why, he drove here in a carriage half an hour ago. A girl with him. That Bona Pittani, the artist. They went in, and I threw a half dollar into the carriage driver to tell me where they came from. He said they'd just been married down at a parsonage around the corner. Good joke on Royce, eh? We'll be the first wedding guests to congratulate the happy pair."

"So she's blackmailed him into marrying her under threats of exposing him as his brother's murderer!" mused Beckwith. "Well, of all the wasted sacrifices! He hates her like poison too."

"But she loves him," amended The Englishman. "And that's just what takes all the pleasure out of the hunt, as far as I'm concerned."

They had reached the door of Ballard's apartments. A man-servant replied to their knock, and, on recognizing the trio, stepped aside to let them enter.

They passed into the little sitting room at the front of the apartment. The Englishman drew back the portières and they filed into the room.

Royce Ballard confronted them almost at the door.

Behind him, half curious, half frightened at the sign of the intruders, stood Bona.

"What does this mean?" asked Ballard sternly.

"Is it a joke?"

"If so, it's on you, Mr. Ballard," answered Gresham. "Let me introduce you to a gentleman whom you already know as Dr. Watts, but whom you may henceforth know as the foremost living detective."

White as death, Ballard recoiled as from some deadly reptile.

CHAPTER XI

A WASTED CRIME

B allard echoed, "The greatest living detective! You surely don't mean Sherlock Holmes?"

"I haven't said so, have I?" said Gresham. "I judge his detective prowess by what I've seen of it. Not by his name."

Ballard, recovering his self-control, turned angrily on The Englishman.

"I do not ask you," he said, "why you have imposed yourself on St. Louis as 'Dr. Watts.' But what I do want to know is, why you have intruded on me at such a time."

"I think you know," replied The Englishman quietly.

The very impassiveness of his tone struck like a chill in Royce's heart.

"I do not know why you are here," he blustered, "and I've no wish to know. Do me a favor to leave. I've met you but once in my life, and I've no desire to prolong the acquaintance."

"You're mistaken, Mr. Ballard. You have met me several times. The last occasion was night before last in Fourth Street. I was obliged to leave you somewhat suddenly, but ..."

"It was you? You who robbed me, and ..."

"It's no use, Mr. Ballard," broke in Gresham, "the game is up."

"Gentlemen," said Bona, who with feminine intuition grasped the whole situation and resolved to play her one card on behalf of the man she loved, "I do not think you quite understand.

"Mr. Ballard and I were married only half an hour ago. It was so soon after his brother's death that the ceremony was private. But I tell you of it in order that you may at least defer business matters until after our honeymoon. It isn't pleasant to have one's wedding trip delayed. Won't you wait – for my sake? It is the custom in my country," she went on, shyly, "to grant any request made by a bride on the day of her wedding. And mine was such a poor, unpretentious little wedding, too! It's hardly fair that the very first persons we announce it to should refuse my very first request – is it?" she ended pleadingly.

Gresham hesitated before the helpless, gentle dignity of her voice and manner.

Beckwith looked uncomfortable.

Even The Englishman seemed reluctant to make any move.

Quick to see the point she had made, the girl went on in the same tone, her hand resting in a light and apparently unconscious caress on Ballard's shoulder.

"You see, my husband has ..."

"Shut up!" growled Royce, shaking himself free from her detaining hand. "This is a plot, and you're in it. You bullied me into marrying you on your threat to cause trouble for me if I refused. And now I find you've sold me out. I ..."

"Hold on, please," interrupted The Englishman, coldly, all his momentary rising sympathy changing to disgust by the brutal words he had just heard.

"I don't like to interfere between man and wife, but you're in error. Miss Pittani – Mrs. Ballard, I should say – did not tell anything. This is the first time I have had the honor of meeting her. What I learned was acquired solely through yourself, Mr. Ballard."

"What you've learned?" sneered Royce, making a last stand. "And what is the wonderful fact that you have learned?"

"The nature and effects of a certain Malay drug known as 'thalesia.'"

For a full minute, Ballard stared at his torturer. His face was void of expression as a Greek mask. It gave no sign of the torrent of thoughts, plans, fears, and final despair that surged through his mind.

At last, with a resigned shrug of the shoulders, Ballard withdrew his fingers from the watch pocket of his white vest, into which they had been carelessly thrust. With a quick gesture, he raised his fingers to his lips.

The Englishman leaped forward to stay him, but he was too late. A spasmodic motion of the throat muscles showed that Ballard had already swallowed whatever he had conveyed to his mouth.

"Thalesia!" exclaimed The Englishman.

"Quite so. There is no antidote," replied Ballard calmly. "According to the formula for the mixture (which I always carried with me, by the way, until after that experience in East St. Louis, when I found a safer hiding place for it) – according to the formula

I have about 15 minutes of life left. I have made a silly bungle of it all. Yes, it was cleverly thought out."

"Don't!" as Bona threw her arms in an agony of fear about him. "Kindly spare me that nonsense in my last moments. What I have just taken was originally meant for you. I always hated you. Did you really think I'd live with you? One of us must have died. It was you or I – and as the dice have fallen the wrong way, it is I."

"I've sent for a doctor," observed The Englishman, who had hurriedly whispered to Gresham, "but it is of no use, as you doubtless know. Still, it may be some slight consolation to you, Mr. Ballard, to know that your intention of murdering your brother stopped short at intention. You did not kill him."

"Did not kill him? But I ..."

"Yes, yes, I know. But you failed. He died in another manner. You are innocent, as far as actual murder goes."

"I suppose I should feel relieved," laughed Royce sardonically, "but somehow I'm not. If you people expect a dramatic and repentant dying scene, you'll be disappointed.

"What I've done, I've done. And I'll take my losses quietly like a man, not like a maudlin fool. I'm not the sort – Great heaven!"

He broke off short in his railing speech.

His face went deathly pallid.

"The formula said it was painless," he screamed.

"Said it was painless – PAINLESS!

"God have mercy! Oh, my God! Mercy!"

Paul Craddock entered his rooms a few days following Royce Ballard's suicide to find The Englishman awaiting him there.

"Hello!" cried Craddock, startled out of his usual composure. "Who let you in?"

"I let myself in," answered The Englishman imperturbably. "I've been here nearly an hour. Ever since I got back from New York. I went there to see a man electrocuted. Not that I cared to see a man killed, but in order to examine the body afterward.

"Thanks to Dr. Irvine's courtesy, I was permitted to do so. It confirmed my own ideas. Do you know, Craddock, it's an interesting thing, this Yankee form of capital punishment of yours? I learned what I wanted to know, namely, that the body of a man who is electrocuted presents the same phenomena as that of a man who has died by a stroke of lightning.

"And a man who has been killed by lightning possesses the same general aspect and organic condition as one who has died of fright. Interesting, is it not? Especially since the coroner's physician declared that poor Cyril Ballard, who fell dead in these rooms, died of fright. Maybe he was electrocuted? Eh?"

Craddock's deep-set eyes were resting on the detective with politely inquiring expression, as though mutely reminding his guest that the latter had not yet explained his outrageous conduct in picking the lock of the rooms and of entering them uninvited in his host's absence.

But The Englishman did not or would not understand the look.

"When I first examined Cyril Ballard's body, the day after I landed in St. Louis," the uninvited guest resumed, "I found a tiny spot on the cushion of the middle finger of his right hand. It was identical, at cursory examination, with a spot I once saw on the chest

of a man who had been struck by lightning. Queer, wasn't it? It gave me an idea, but the idea seemed so wildly improbable that I couldn't believe it plausible. And yet," he added, reflectively, "I ought by this time to know that it is only the seemingly probable things in crime which are really improbable.

"May I offer you a cigarette? No? Well, an easier more probable clew offered itself, and I've wasted much time following it, but I've come to the worthless end of it at last. It ended in the body of a suicide with a heart-wrecked woman weeping over it. So I am back on the old, original, seemingly improbable trail again. And, strangely enough, it has led me here.

"I owe you an apology, Mr. Craddock, for secretly entering your rooms for the purpose of spying. But, as my quest has brought me perfect success, I cannot feel as sorry as I should."

"Dr. Watts," began Craddock, angrily, "it ..."

"Excuse me, Mr. Craddock," politely interposed the other, "but I see no further reason for concealing my identity from you. Permit me to apologize for deceiving you so long as to my identity and to introduce myself to you by my own name."

And he did so.

Craddock opened his lips to speak, but it was The Englishman who spoke first.

"Mr. Craddock," he said politely, "would you mind telling me what was your motive in murdering Cyril Ballard?"

If The Englishman had expected that Craddock would express surprise, consternation or denial, he was disappointed.

Paul Craddock's stern, semi-classic features underwent no change. The politely bored look did not leave his eyes.

"Why did you kill Cyril Ballard?" repeated The Englishman.

"Is that any concern of yours?" asked Craddock, coldly. "The question strikes me as impertinent. Yet, something is due you perhaps, in reward for the skill you've shown in discovering that I killed him. But for you, I would never have been suspected. Yet I am not wholly sorry you have solved the mystery. I am tired of St. Louis. One of my old, restless fits has been on me for some time. I had already planned to journey again to some distant corner of the world for a few years. You are simply forcing me to go a little earlier than I had expected to."

"I am afraid," said The Englishman, regretfully (for he had acquired a keen liking and respect for the man) "that your journey this time will carry you further afield than ever before and that your ticket will include no return privileges. You see, the law kills people for premeditated murder."

"And you know me so little as to imagine I would allow myself to be taken? No, no, my friend! And I shall not even make a fool of myself by committing suicide like poor Royce Ballard. Life still holds much for me. I shall be long dead. If I have my way, I shall also be long living."

Without perceptible emotion, Craddock turned from the mantle against which he had been leaning. In his right hand shone a revolver. The muzzle was on a line with The Englishman's head. The distance was barely six feet. There was no missing at that range – there was nothing melodramatic in the man's action.

"Yes," went on Craddock in the same tone, "I have nothing to fear from the law nor from you. It would cause me considerable regret to kill you because I've taken a liking to you. But if it comes to your life or mine, I need not tell you the outcome."

The Englishman saw he was covered, that the slightest self-defensive move on his part must mean swift death; that his antagonist was no ordinary criminal, but possessed a nerve of iron and a wit and indomitable purpose to match.

"It's your move, Mr. Craddock" he replied after a brief pause.

"Good. I ask you to give me your word not to attempt to molest me in any way. If you do so, you may stay here while I make my preparations for departure, and I will even go so far as to answer any questions you may care to ask. I beg you will accept my terms. For the alternative would be painful to us both."

A moment's hesitation and The Englishman's mind was made up. This was a man of his word, a man in a thousand; a man on whom any attempted subterfuge might fail.

CHAPTER XII

VICTOR OR VANQUISHED?

The Englishman agreed at length. "I accept your terms," he said. "I am not wholly sorry to do so, for it would have cost me some sorrow to cause the arrest and subsequent death of a man who had so often been my host, and who has shown me so much kindness. Let me take advantage of your promise to answer my questions.

"I will begin by repeating my first query. Why did you kill Cyril Ballard?"

Craddock had pocketed the pistol at The Englishman's first words of assurance and was now moving about the rooms collecting various necessary articles with the alert skill of a practiced packer and tossing them into a suitcase.

"I did not mean to kill him at all," he answered at last. "I intended to kill Siurd Von Rickerl."

The Englishman raised his eyebrows in slight surprise. He now recalled having heard that Craddock was once reported to be deeply in love with Iris Durand. She had preferred Von Rickerl. The Englishman could readily understand how a man of Craddock's sort might not scruple to remove from his path the one obstacle to his happiness.

"And now," resumed Craddock, "may I ask a favor in return for the information I have given you? I still have a few minutes before I need to start for my train. I have often heard of the way famous detectives track down criminals.

"Will you kindly outline for me the method you used in my case? It will be something for me to remember – to have had you explain to me in person your mode of work."

A slight smile, quickly suppressed, attested The Englishman's appreciation of the compliment. In a few sentences, he recounted his pursuit of Royce Ballard from start to finish. Then he continued:

"Failing in fixing the murder on him, I reverted to my first theory; namely, that Cyril died of electric shock. I have already explained to you my reasons for that theory; the burnt spot on the finger, the expression of face, etc. I went to Sing Sing where I examined the body of a man who had just been electrocuted. I learned from that examination that I was right in believing Cyril Ballard had been electrocuted. But how?

"That necessitated a search of your rooms. My first move, after letting myself in here, was to examine the alcove where the piano stands. I merely moved the piano a few inches from the wall in the course of my search, and there the whole secret was revealed. It saved me the trouble of any further deduction. The rest was mere child's play."

"Go on," suggested Craddock, as The Englishman paused. "It will be interesting to know how near the truth you come."

"I found at the back of the piano a group of electric wires, issuing apparently from the body of the instrument and passing through the wall behind. I went around to the room on the opposite side of the wall. It is a mere closet with an electric switchboard whereby the lighting of the various rooms of your apartment is regulated. A very few moments' study showed me that the wires had been arranged so as to throw all the electric current into the piano.

"Later these connecting wires had been cut close to the wall. Let me give you my idea of the killing. You in some way arranged that, by a turn of the switch, a strong current should be thrown into the piano. On the night of Cyril Ballard's death, you got Siurd Von Rickerl headed safely for the piano, then slipped in here and turned on the switch. You could not foresee that Cyril Ballard would push in ahead and seat himself on the piano stool. Later, when you discovered your error, you came back in here, tried to turn off the switch, found it jammed and so cut the wires. The brass work on the board is scratched, showing how hard you tugged in your effort to turn back the switch. Am I right?"

"Entirely," affirmed Craddock, deeply interested.

"Go on."

"Then I examined the piano, and I saw how the whole thing had been done. You connected one electric pole with the loud pedal. Then, boring through the ivory key of 'G natural' below high C, you ran a metal wire through it connecting with the opposite electric pole. You filed down the wire to a level with the key.

"By the dim lamplight, it would be practically invisible. But, when the current was on, anyone pressing down the loud pedal and striking that note with great force would form what is known as a 'short circuit.' The whole electric current would rush through his body, causing instant death. It was a clever idea. I congratulate you on its conception, fatal though it was. It is the cleverest scheme that has ever come under my somewhat wide range of experience."

Craddock bowed.

"Is that the extent of your discovery?" he asked.

"Not quite. When Cyril Ballard struck that death chord, it drew off for the moment all the electric power in the apartment. As a result, every light in the place went out. You had not counted on that, eh? Then, when you slipped into the next room and cut the wires, the circuit was, of course, momentarily shut off again. The room was plunged into darkness. The metal strings of the piano, strongly impregnated by the tremendous electric force that had been turned into them, had contracted as the striking of that chord had sent the current into the piano. As the wires were cut, the current ceased. The strings suddenly relaxing, of course, caused that identical chord to be struck once more, although no one was ever near the instrument.

"It is a simple and old electric piano trick. But it accounts for the moment of darkness and the repetition of that one crashing death chord. There is the whole story. Mr. Craddock. Good day."

Craddock stretched forth his hand.

"It is a privilege to have met you, sir," he said, almost cordially. "I shall be honored by shaking your hand."

The Englishman eyed the proffered hand without making any move to grasp it.

"You will pardon me, I am sure," he answered, apologetically, half sadly, "but even a detective must draw the line between his admiration for a murderer's skill and his personal loathing of that murderer's crime. You will understand my feeling, I am sure, when I decline to ..."

"Don't mention it," returned Craddock coldly, though a faint flush rose to his dark face as his rejected hand dropped back to his side. "Good-by."

"Now, I wonder," mused The Englishman, as he strolled contemplatively down Grand Avenue, on leaving the Odeon, "I wonder if this Ballard affair, taken all in all, should rank as one of my triumphs or one of my rare defeats?"

Half a block farther on he met Gresham.

"The case is wound up, Gresham," said The Englishman. "Tomorrow I set out for London. There is no longer any reason why I should conceal my identity. Do you still want to know my real name? Yes? Well, let's drop into this café and have a highball. Over the drinks, I'll tell you who I really am."

THE THEATER

THE EDITOR

THE AUTHOR

ABOUT THE ODEON THEATER
AND THE
MASONIC TEMPLE

William Albert Swasey (October 11, 1863 – March 21, 1940), the designer of the Odeon Theater in St. Louis, was born in Melbourne, Australia, where his father's firm, J. B. Swasey Commission Company, had offices. He studied architecture at Massachusetts Institute of Technology, graduating from there in 1882.

Following graduation from M.I.T., Mr. Swasey worked for C. C. Height in New York, and then for Burnham & Root and Henry Ives Cobb in Chicago. He located to St. Louis in 1885 and formed a partnership with Charles K. Ramsey. Swasey opened his own office in 1887 and his designs, from St. Louis to Memphis to Pittsburgh, appeared regularly in architectural journals. Swasey designed the Pastime Athletic Club in St. Louis, along with numerous homes in the prestige areas of Westmoreland Place, Portland Place, and Westminster Place, a private street for which he was commissioned to design the entrance gates.

In early 1899 *The Brickbuilder* reported Swasey had received a commission for a ten-story building in New Orleans. In the August, 1899, issue it was reported that he had also received a commission for a similar structure in Memphis. It also reported that:

"Mr. Swasey is doing much to advance the interests of St. Louis. He is progressive, learned, has advanced thoughts and ideas on architecture, and is one of the foremost architects of the country."

In 1899, the Masonic Building and Musical Theater Company gave the commission for the Odeon Theater complex at 1038 North Grand Avenue (at Bell) to architect Albert W. Swasey. The Odeon complex, which was of Italian Renaissance design cost $400,000 and consisted of two sections. The front section was a five-story building designed for Masonic lodge functions, while the theater was a building toward the rear with a street level entrance.

The Odeon was designed to be a musical theater; it had seating for 2,000 people and was noted for its outstanding acoustical properties. It was comprised of the auditorium which had a large stage and a 40-foot-high proscenium arch; a parlor seating 200, rehearsal hall, studio rooms, and a music library. The Odeon also had two through driveways in the basement of the theater that allowed passengers to be dropped off inside the building.

The first live production at the Odeon Theater was November 28, 1899. Within a year the St. Louis Symphony had adopted this new theater as its home and remained there for the next 35 years.

In 1926, the Masonic Temple moved from the Odeon's North Grand location to the new Temple on Lindell. In 1934, the St. Louis Symphony moved to a different location, and, in 1935, the Odeon was destroyed by two fires.

After the turn of the century, Mr. Swasey went on to design two other theaters in St. Louis. In 1902 he moved to New York where he associated with the Schubert brothers and designed more than a dozen theaters in and around New York City.

ABOUT THE EDITOR
TRUDY THOMAS MONTEITH

Trudy Thomas Monteith is a retired legal assistant who lives in St. Louis, Missouri with her husband, Harry Monteith. A Certified Professional Secretary, her career spanned 50 years during which time she served as assistant to the General Counsel of a Fortune 500 company and assistant to the Chairs of two of St. Louis's most prestigious law firms. Having graduated from Saint Louis Community College, she also attended University College-Washington University in St. Louis and Lindenwood College.

Trudy served as National Secretary of the Society of American Magicians for 10 years and is currently serving as Midwest Regional Vice President of the Society. She is also a Trustee of the S.A.M. Magic Endowment Fund, a position she has held for 25 years. Trudy and her husband are known in the "magic world" as Harry and Trudy Monti. She is currently researching the history of magic in St. Louis. Her works include:

- *The Fatal Chord, or the Baffling Mystery of the Odeon Murder* (editor, 2023)
- *The Fatal Chord, or the Baffling Mystery of the Carnegie Hall Murder* (editor, 2023)
- *The History of Society of American Magicians Assembly 8* (author, 1996)
- *The Magic of Fat-Free Cooking* (author, 1996)

109

ABOUT THE AUTHOR
ALBERT PAYSON TERHUNE

Albert Payson Terhune (December 21, 1872 – February 18, 1942) was an American journalist who was popular for his novels relating to his favorite collies.

He received a Bachelor of Arts degree in 1893 from Columbia University. From 1894 to 1916, he worked as a reporter for *The Evening World*, a New York newspaper that was published from 1887 to 1931 and served as the evening edition of the *New York World*.

Mr. Terhune initially published short stories about Lad, his collie, in various general interest magazines such as *Saturday Evening Post* and *Ladies' Home Journal*. His first book was a collection of stories about Lad and was followed by over 30 additional dog-focused novels, including two about Lad.

Regarding *The Fatal Chord, or the Baffling Mystery of the Carnegie Hall Murder*, as of May 15, 2023, the website *Historical & Fictional Characters in Sherlockian Pastiches* indicates that it has not been published since 1904 and was not published as a book, nor is it listed in the following *Wikipedia* list of Mr. Terhune's publications:

- *Syria from the Saddle* (1896)
- *Columbia Stories* (1897)
- *How to Box to Win* (1900) (written as "Terry McGovern")

- *Dr. Dale: A Story Without a Moral* (1900) (with Marion Harland)
- *The New Mayor* (1907)
- *Caleb Conover, Railroader* (1907)
- *The World's Great Events* (1908)
- *The Fighter* (1909)
- *The Return of Peter Grimm* (1912, novelization of the play by David Belasco)
- *The Woman* (1912)
- *Famous American Indians* (1912)
- *Around the World in Thirty Days* (1914)
- *Dad* (1914) (with Sinclair Lewis)
- *The Story of Damon and Pythias* (1915)
- *The Red Circle* novelization (1915)
- *Superwomen* (1916) republished as *Famous Hussies of History* (1943)
- *Dollars and Cents* (1917)
- *The Years of the Locust* (1917)
- *Fortune* (1918)
- *Wonder Women In History* (1918)
- *Lad: A Dog* (1919)
- *Bruce* (1920)
- *Buff: A Collie* (1921)
- *The Man in the Dark* (1921)
- *His Dog* (1922)
- *Black Gold* (1922)
- *Black Caesar's Clan* (1922)
- *Further Adventures of Lad* (1922) republished as *Dog Stories Every Child Should Know* (1941)
- *The Pest* (1923)
- *Lochinvar Luck* (1923)
- *The Amateur Inn* (1923)

- *Grudge Mountain* (1923) republished as *Dog of the High Sierras* (Grosset & Dunlap)
- *Treve* (1924)
- *The Tiger's Claw* (1924)
- *The Heart of a Dog* (1924)
- *Now That I'm Fifty* (1924)
- *The Runaway Bag* (1925)
- *Wolf* (1925)
- *Najib* (1925)
- *Treasure* (1926) republished as *The Faith of a Collie* (1949)
- *My Friend the Dog* (1926)
- *Gray Dawn* (1927)
- *The Luck of the Laird* (1927) republished as *A Highland Collie* (1950)
- *Bumps* (1927)
- *Blundell's Last Guest* (1927)
- *Water!* (1928)
- *Black Wings* (1928)
- *Loot* (1928) republished as *Collie to the Rescue* (1940)
- *The Secret of Sea-Dream House* (1929)
- *Lad of Sunnybank* (1929)
- *To the Best of My Memory* (1930)
- *Diana Thorne's Dog Basket: A Series of Etchings* (1930)
- *Proving Nothing* (1930)
- *A Dog Named Chips* (1931)
- *The Son of God* (1932)
- *The Dog Book* (1932)
- *The Way of a Dog* (1932)
- *Letters of Marque* (1934)
- *The Book of Sunnybank* (1934) republished as *Sunnybank: Home of Lad* (1953)
- *Real Tales of Real Dogs* (1935)
- *True Dog Stories* (1936)

- *The Critter and Other Dogs* (1936)
- *Unseen!* (1937)
- *The Terhune Omnibus* (1937) republished as *The Best-Loved Dog Stories of Albert Payson Terhune* (1954)
- *A Book of Famous Dogs* (1937) republished as *Famous Dog Stories Every Child Should Know* (1937)
- *Grudge Mountain* (1939) republished as *Dog of the High Sierras* (1951)
- *Dogs* (1940)
- *Loot!* (1940) republished as *Collie to the Rescue* (1952)
- *Across the Line* (1945) (notes/commentary by Anice Terhune)
- *Wallace: Glasgow's Immortal Fire Dog* (1961)
- *Great Dog Stories* (1994) five stories from *The Heart of a Dog* and five stories from *My Friend the Dog*

Made in the USA
Monee, IL
15 September 2023

42739186R00069